Noel, Alabama

Noel, Alabama

An Alabama Christmas Romance

Susan Sands

TULE
PUBLISHING

Dear Reader,

Every book "becomes" amidst a unique set of circumstances. *Noel, Alabama* began as an idea tucked away in a file and pulled out as I sat in the surgical waiting area of Northside Hospital in Atlanta while my mom underwent major back surgery.

The development of this story happened as I spent my days bedside while my mom drifted in and out and I advocated fiercely for better pain control. I watched all the Lifetime holiday movies because the choices were limited at the hospital. I write this to tell you how this book came to be.

I want to thank Meghan Farrell at Tule for her vision and patience with this story and with me. Thanks to Jane Porter for greenlighting another Alabama book. As always, so much appreciation goes to my brilliant editor, Sinclair Sawhney, who continues to champion my writing and make me look good.

Thanks to Brad Arnold, Hollywood producer, and all-around great human. Brad spoon fed me the terminology and knowledge for all things movie making in this story.

The last half of writing this book was spent under strict quarantine with both my husband and my college daughter at home. So, my process wasn't the normal one. I worried my way to the last word, about my mom and so many others. About how our world will become in the short and long term.

Thanks to my husband, Doug, for all the grocery runs. And my adult kids for supporting me.

This one is a little different, but I'll let my readers determine how so.

Enjoy this coming home, second chances love story set in Ministry, Alabama.

All the best!
Susan Sands

Chapter One

"ANYBODY GOT AN idea here? Anybody at all?" Mr. Stone, the location manager for the film, and Bailey's boss, yelled. His face was beet red, almost as red as his skinny pants. He had a yellow sweater tied around his neck, where the veins popped out prominently.

Bailey, Jem, and Alexis, along with a handful of other assistant producers, directors, and higher-ups sat, all tense, because the worse-case scenario had befallen them.

The director, Brad, was equally red in the face. This meeting wasn't going well. "Since we've spent a couple million dollars already to shoot this picture, only to lose our location because of—" The director's disgust could be felt like a wave throughout the room.

The reason they'd lost their filming location was the singular fault of a minor actor's amorous exploits with the mayor's wife in the town where they'd been shooting the project. The mayor had kicked them out, effective immediately, using a clause in the contract where he'd found a decency loophole, and that, as they say in the business, had been a wrap.

Bailey, as assistant location manager, somehow felt as if she should *do* something, even though losing their Christmas location smack in the middle of filming wasn't anything to do with her.

Before the idea was fully formed, and as the knot formed in her belly, Bailey stood and spoke, not nearly as loudly or confidently as she'd hoped. "I've got a place for us—I think. I might be able to fix this. Give me a week to see if I can work it out."

All heads turned and eyes fixed on Bailey. *Oh God. She would have to go back to Ministry, Alabama.* She would have to go home. "My hometown in Alabama. It's the most Christmas-y of all the Christmas places you've ever been. The gigantic tree in the town square rivals Rockefeller Center, I swear."

The producer, who'd sat quietly stewing throughout the meeting, skewered her with a stare. "You've got a week to secure lodging for all of us, plus the trailers, and base camp. Stone will fill you in." He indicated with a dismissive hand to her pinched-lipped boss.

Now she'd done it. There was no going back.

⟫⟪

"ARE YOU SURE this is going to work?" Alexis asked. "Sounds like you put yourself in a pickle if it doesn't."

"I'm almost sure," Bailey said, biting her lip. But there were so many reasons she personally rebelled against the entire idea of it. "I mean, I think I can get what I need back home for the scenes we still have to shoot. They're all exterior, so that should give us some flexibility."

"But Alabama." Alexis made a face.

"Yeah, you have no idea. But not for the obvious reasons," Bailey said.

"Sounds like heading back home isn't your first choice." Alexis raised her eyebrows in question. "Do tell."

"Long story. But it will be great to see my daddy."

"Oh, that sounds charming. *Daddy.* Kind of like *Gone with the Wind.* I can't wait to meet him." Alexis was a friend, and Bailey was thankful she would be joining her on this adventure home.

"You'll love Ministry. If only for the shock value and the pizza."

"Pizza?"

"Best pizza you've ever had."

"Can't wait."

BAILEY BOONE PULLED open one of the two impressive old leaded glass doors of the Ministry Inn and nearly dropped her Tumi carry-on roller bag at the unexpected, and very loud jingling of bells that knocked against the glass.

Did they still hang bells from the doors of every business in this town? Clearly it *was* still a thing here in Ministry, Alabama. Or maybe it was only for Christmas. Because it was December first, which meant Ministry was decked out in its full holiday finery, from streetlights wrapped like candy canes to the faux snow sprayed around the edges of every store front in town, despite the questionably fall-ish temps in the South. But that could change on a dime around here, and Bailey prayed it would for her selfish purposes.

That's exactly why she'd landed back here. Christmas. Not the holiday as much as the décor. And the many, many red and green activities Ministry had to offer in the coming weeks. Bailey required a town where Christmas abounded. And there was none better than her hometown. Coming back here had been out of pure necessity—job related of course. Bailey was on a mission to get her long-awaited and much-deserved promotion.

The price: returning to the place she'd mostly avoided during her adult life. This meant dealing with Seth McKay, for one. And coming back home, where she would definitely run into all the people she'd known in her previous life. It would all be—awkward—and Bailey hated awkward.

She'd dragged her suitcase here from the car, the wheels of which normally rolled as smooth as glass. But they hadn't, of course, because she'd been forced to park in a gravel lot on the other side of the town square. The parking area in front of the Ministry Inn was filled with cars. Well, trucks mostly. Ones with big tires. Must be the lunch crowd at the pizza joint next door.

Bailey smoothed her hair, hoping her outward appearance didn't yet reflect her inward annoyed and frustrated self. Today was a big one, and she had a lot to do in a short amount of time. It was probably too much to ask to slip in and not be recognized by anyone until she'd accomplished at least some of the things on her list.

"Bailey Boone! So glad you made it." She didn't flinch or react. Being around actors, Bailey had picked up a thing or two. So, being wrapped in a surprisingly strong hug as she'd stepped inside, had Bailey slapping on a smile like it happened every day.

The unexpected hugger was a woman about her size, whom she'd known her entire life. And if Bailey were honest, a welcome face, and a helpful one, so the hug wasn't completely *un*welcome.

Bailey's smile turned genuine, and she greeted Cammie warmly. "It's great to see you, Cammie. Thanks for your help getting this arranged at the last minute. You're a lifesaver," Bailey said. Cammie was her contact here in setting all this up.

"Pretty exciting that you're gonna bring Hollywood to our little town." Cammie starred in a top-rated Southern cooking show shot right here in Ministry, Alabama, so she was no stranger to the camera herself.

"Nothing new for you, I'd guess, but we're going to disrupt things around here quite a lot. I hope the residents don't get too bent out of shape." Bailey's job as a location assistant for a big Hollywood studio regularly brought her to out-of-the-way towns that hadn't been exposed to such things. But never to her own hometown.

Cammie laughed. "Oh, they're split about fifty-fifty. Half are starstruck and the other half are already grousing about how it's going to ruin *everything*. Just giving you a heads-up."

"I do this for a living. I'm used to the reactions from locals," Bailey said. She expected some pushback from the older crowd especially. "Once they realize how much extra business we bring with us, they'll get on board. For the most part," Bailey said. "The whole town gets a shot in the arm from this. Well, most of it anyway."

"Yes, but you've known most of these people your whole life," Cammie said. "They're a stubborn bunch." The eye roll made Bailey smile a little. The words were so true.

"Yes. My whole life." Bailey thought a minute about that. Both women stared out the large plate glass windows of the inn at the picturesque downtown. "It's as beautiful as I remember." Nobody did Christmas like Ministry. From the enormous tree that really did rival the one at Rockefeller Center in New York City to the decorations that graced every square inch of—*everything*. Lucky for Bailey, the festivities were only the beginning, so the timing was perfect for the many outdoor scenes they had left to shoot.

Fortunately, they'd wrapped up the indoor scenes before the "falling out" with the other location.

This left the studio in a budget deficit and without a

place to film the rest of the exterior Christmas scenes on location. She'd reached out to Cammie first because they were friends who still managed to keep in contact through social media.

Cammie agreed to help immediately, but when Bailey had learned that the mayor, Ben Laroux, was out of town, and she'd have to deal with the sheriff, Seth McKay (yes, that Seth McKay), Bailey had to admit she'd paused momentarily before moving forward. It might even have been easier to simply stop things at that point and tell the exalted Mr. Stone that things just weren't going to pan out.

But since she'd worked so hard to get to this point, she couldn't let Seth be the obstacle who prevented her from moving to the next level in her career. Nope. No way.

Seth McKay, who she'd left behind as she'd flown off to film school in California at age eighteen. Sadly, they'd both been heartbroken fools at the time. But Bailey had needed more than what Ministry had to offer. There had been a million reasons to leave, but only one to stay. She'd had big dreams that couldn't be fulfilled here. Or Alabama.

Bailey hadn't looked back. She'd made a clean break with Seth and insisted he not wait around for her. There would be no long-distance relationship. Seth wasn't the L.A. kind of guy. That dog wouldn't hunt. In fact, she couldn't have imagined him anywhere but here. And here, he still was.

So she would definitely have to pay the price for ambition. The price being a whopping dose of her past smacking her right in the face. Bailey had no idea how Seth would react to her coming back here and inserting herself into his daily routine.

Maybe twelve years had completely cured him of their past.

Maybe it had cured her.

But she had a job to do, so nothing could get in the way of that. Right now, this very minute, it was time to find lodging for upward of fifty people who would be arriving soon. She wasn't completely sure how to pull that off, but the inn was a start now that she'd scored the perfect filming location. Yes, she'd done some online research, and called around to the hotels right outside of town. Problem was, Ministry wasn't like most places. Folks here preferred to do business in person.

She'd dealt with places like Ministry before, but never on such short notice only weeks before Christmas. Normally, these things were meticulously set up and organized months in advance.

Ministry had put itself on the map in recent years for its Christmas festival offerings, not to mention *Cammie's Down-Home Cooking* show that filmed here. There was a restaurant and a connected store that sold memorabilia and cookbooks. So, it really was the perfect spot for saving the film.

It would work for the characters to play out their stories while attending the town's many planned holiday activities.

There was a 5K Jingle Jog, a Christmas pageant, a tour of historical homes, a cookie-baking contest and treat swap, and ornament decorating that culminated with placing them on the tree in the square. The ceremonial tree lighting was a big one, of course, but that would happen before the cast and crew arrived, unfortunately.

Honestly, Bailey couldn't remember all of them. She'd have to consult her list. But there were plenty of opportunities that coincided with the original script. This prevented the writers and directors from having to change too many of the established scenes.

"Well, I'd better get back to shooting my own show or Matthew will have my hide," Cammie said. "I wanted to pop by and welcome you home."

"Thanks so much, and tell Matthew how much I appreciate his helping to get this done on such short notice," Bailey said. Matthew Pope was Cammie's producer, and together they'd been key in pulling this all together. Bailey would be forever grateful, and if all went as she hoped, this might be the save that would get her bumped up to location manager when Mr. Stone retired. *If* he ever retired.

"Don't mention it. We were glad to help. It'll be fun to see Ministry on the big screen. Call me if you need anything," Cammie said. "Oh, and don't forget to stop by Seth's office next door and work out all the details for setup. Ben won't be back until late next week." Cammie breezed out after dropping that bomb. Ben Laroux, the mayor, was

Cammie's twin brother.

Bailey nearly groaned out loud. She didn't need that reminder. It wasn't only Seth that had her avoiding Ministry. There were other reasons she'd been keen on leaving as soon as humanly possible as a young woman. The reasons were many and varied. And complicated. Bailey simply wasn't like the other girls in Ministry. She'd cared nothing for dresses and makeup. She could go on.

Bailey realized her thoughts were going to a place that were unhelpful at present, so she straightened her shoulders and refocused.

It was the reward for her education and endless struggle since leaving. Yes, it had been a stressful climb from gofer to location assistant at Epic Films, but so worth it now that she'd gotten this far. While hers didn't sound especially impressive, there was a heavy burden of responsibility attached to that assistant title. She was in charge of scouting the location before the manager to prepare for the arrival of the talent and the film crew. She had to secure lodging and pave the way for Mr. Stone, as he was the big-picture person. He insisted they call him Mr. Stone, though it wasn't always what they called him when he wasn't in the room. No matter. Pleasing Mr. Stone would be her stepping*stone* to his job once he decided she was ready.

If that meant dealing with Seth McKay, the one person who'd nearly been her downfall, then so be it. She hoped he had a soft belly now; maybe he'd lost some hair. That would make it easier. She *might* have passed his office on the way in. But she'd dared not look.

Once, when she'd come home at Christmas, she'd seen Seth with her best friend. He had been kissing her under a piece of mistletoe during the tree lighting in the square. Bailey hadn't bothered saying hello.

⟫⟪

SHE WAS BACK. Seth McKay had spotted Bailey Boone dragging some fancy suitcase past his office window twenty minutes ago. Someone might as well have punched him right in the gut. He'd tried not to react since Cheryl, the chief of police, sat at her desk not fifty feet from his. And she was unlikely to let him live it down should he make an idiot of himself over the return of his high school girlfriend. Well, she'd been more than that, since they'd known one another their whole lives.

Cammie Laroux had warned him that Bailey was headed here just ahead of a full movie crew and slew of actors and other Hollywood types to film some scenes from a Christmas feature film.

Bailey looked fantastic from what he could tell as she whizzed by, with her aviator sunglasses, jeans tucked into black boots, and white sweater with a plaid scarf slung around her neck. Her hair was the same; chestnut brown with those blond streaks. He was glad she hadn't changed it. But she was chic, slick. Casual Hollywood. She had an intimidating bearing. All five-foot-four inches of her.

She'd moved past with confidence, like a woman in charge. The Bailey he'd known so well until she'd blown out of here at eighteen had been—complicated. And sweet and funny. She'd been everything to him back then.

Seth had heard she'd buzzed into town several times over the years but oddly he'd missed seeing her. Somehow he'd doubted that had been an accident. A town this size left little room for outmaneuvering a run-in with someone unless it was by design.

Hearing that Bailey Boone was coming back to Ministry for an extended period of time had been something of a shocker. Not that he believed anything Bailey did at this point in her life had anything to do with him. Still, he had to admit that learning of her impending arrival stirred up some pretty mixed emotions.

They would meet again; it was imminent. In fact, it was necessary and needed to be soon. Since the mayor was out of town, that left the important details of welcoming the incoming visitors and getting everyone settled to Seth. He was Bailey's point man, as it were, and whether either of them liked it or not, they had business together.

Chapter Two

WHEN THE BELLS jingled on yet another door she opened, Bailey wasn't quite as surprised as she'd been the first time. It was a sound from her past. Maybe that's why it irritated her. And as she entered the Okaloosa County Sheriff's Office, which shared space with the Ministry Police Department, Bailey took a deep breath and intentionally pulled up her chin so as not to avoid anyone's eyes.

There he was. Seth McKay in the flesh. Tipped back in his office chair, jean-encased legs and boots crossed on his great big mahogany desk, perusing a newspaper, not a device like most folks in L.A., as if he hadn't a care in the world. He hadn't even looked up when she'd entered.

No, he hadn't lost his hair. And judging by how his shoulders filled out the khaki button-down, county-issued shirt, he'd not developed a gut either. Bailey was torn, and somewhat annoyed. Should she clear her throat or stomp her feet to get his attention?

"Bailey Boone, as I live and breathe. It's been a minute since we've seen you around here. Welcome home."

Bailey had been so fixed on her throwback man-target,

she'd missed the woman sitting on the other side of the room at a desk just outside her periphery.

"Oh, hi. Thank you. It's great to see you again, Cheryl." Cheryl Hodges wore a uniform that was blue and gray with a badge pinned on the lapel. Bailey and Cheryl had gone to school together growing up. They'd been friends but hadn't stayed in touch. Bailey hadn't stayed in touch with anyone besides Cammie on social media. She'd had quite a few requests from others in town, but she hadn't responded. Once, when she had, they'd wanted to know how to get into the movie business. So, Bailey decided not to engage.

"I hear you're dragging this town into the spotlight whether we like it or not," Cheryl said. Bailey couldn't decipher whether or not Cheryl believed that to be a good thing.

Bailey kept one eye on Seth, who'd still not looked up.

"I'm hoping it's a good thing. I plan to help things run as smoothly as possible," Bailey said.

"Well, we're here to assist you in any way we can; *aren't we, Sheriff?*" Cheryl said a little too loudly.

They both swung their gazes toward the man hiding behind his newspaper in the back corner of the room.

The newspaper lowered slowly.

Bailey was skewered with an ice-cold blue gaze. "I reckon we are. Welcome back to Ministry, Bailey Boone."

Bailey's heart nearly beat out of her chest. "Good to see you again, Seth."

"I've got to go out and check on some coffee. Y'all want anything?" Cheryl asked as she clipped her sidearm to her belt. Cheryl was no fool.

"Not for me, thanks," Bailey said.

"I'm good," Seth said.

The door bells jingled as they continued to stare at one another.

"So, you're really back?" He'd managed to lower his newspaper and his feet.

Bailey swallowed a Captain Obvious remark and nodded. Now that he was sitting upright, she could see that he was quite fit. In fact, he'd filled out, but she'd bet money there wasn't an ounce of fat on him anywhere.

"You look good, Bailey," he said, his gaze direct and un-blinking.

Bailey worked to hold his stare. "Thanks. So do you." It was true, but she hated that she'd noticed and been so affected by the fact.

"Where are you staying?" he asked.

Bailey didn't have a good answer for that one. "I-I'm not sure yet. I'm working on getting lodging for all the cast and crew. This change of venue has happened so quickly, I haven't figured out my situation yet."

"What about Aames? He'd be thrilled to have you," Seth said.

Yes, her daddy would love that. "I wish I could stay with him, but he's too far from the center of town. I need to be within shouting distance to the action." If she were staying outside of town at her daddy's house, it would put her at a disadvantage if she was needed in a pinch. "Plus, the cell service out in the woods is iffy."

"Gotcha." He nodded in the general direction of the street. "Maybe you should check with Mrs. Wiggins."

Mrs. Wiggins, if she remembered correctly, was a tiny older lady who owned the historical Victorian home across the street in the center of downtown. "Does she rent rooms now?" When Bailey had lived here in Ministry, she did not. In fact, Bailey had a memory of Mrs. Wiggins's grandchildren running around her tiny yard.

"Mrs. Wiggins has turned her home into four apartments for short- or long-term renters. They're very nice, with high ceilings and big windows, and a view of downtown. She doesn't have any renters right now. She's extremely picky about who she allows into her home because she still lives downstairs. Personally, I think she only does it for the company when she's in the mood."

Bailey smiled at that thought. How nice to live to be a certain age and have that kind of choice, depending on your mood. "I'll check and see what the status is with her apartments."

"You might also try Evangeline House since they're only a few blocks away. Mrs. Laroux remarried and lives with her husband, Howard. They've added a B&B in addition to the event planning business."

Bailey had pulled out her notebook and was scribbling away. "This is very helpful. Thank you, Seth." She looked up, realizing anew to whom she spoke. Those darn blue eyes gave her a kick before she could protect herself. He was older now, of course, but twelve years had done nothing to diminish his good looks. He was her age—thirty.

"I took an oath to serve and protect," he grinned as he said the words.

And those dimples. She knew he wasn't married based on the intel fed to her by Daddy and Cammie. But Bailey did wonder how he'd gone this long in a woman-saturated town like Ministry without getting hitched. Yes, she knew he'd dated here and there, but never married.

"You've done well here, Seth. I'm happy for you." She meant it. In fact, it would've made her happier if she'd come back and he'd been joyfully married with a half dozen kids. His being single, well, that was more complicated. Not *actually* complicated, more in her head than in reality.

"And look at you, Miz Hollywood. This job. It's everything you dreamed of when you left." He smiled as he said, it but there were some unspoken things in his words, and in his eyes as he held her gaze.

Bailey wasn't going anywhere near that. She pretended not to notice the underlying angst. Instead she stayed with the superficial. "It's been a climb for sure. I started as the lowest gopher on the set and have worked my way up. So, yes, Hollywood has been an adventure."

"I'm glad you've made your dreams come true." He let that hang there.

"Thanks." She let that hang there.

Now it was getting beyond awkward. "So, how's your momma?" Bailey asked, because she did want to know. Joella McKay held a special place in Bailey's heart and always would. When Bailey'd left Ministry at such a young age, she'd missed Joella almost as much as she had Daddy and Seth.

He smiled. "She's great. Same as ever. Owns the Pizza Pie now. Pizza Joe passed last year and left it to her. She was as surprised as anybody when the attorney called her into the reading of the will and told her. But anybody with half a brain knew Joe was crazy about her." The old man had always seen Joella as the daughter he'd never had. She'd worked there and helped him run the place for years.

"Oh, wow. That's great. I'll have to stop in and say hello." The Pizza Pie had been around as long as anyone could remember. It was the only pizza establishment in the downtown area and did a steady business year-round. But Pizza Joe didn't have a lick of family. It was great to know his business and legacy would carry on.

"She would love that." His smile was genuine, but there was something else; it was the easy grin she remembered so well, but he kind of smirked like he knew something she didn't.

"What?" she asked, in reference to his expression.

He shook his head but said by way of explanation, "It's nice to see you, Bailey."

The old familiarity threatened to overwhelm her. That tug in his voice, the face she hadn't seen in so many years. *God, how she'd missed him.* He wasn't the wiry boy anymore, but he was still the same Seth.

No! She couldn't allow herself to get sucked back in by his easy manner and charm. "So who do I speak with about filming our scenes during the next couple weeks? I'll need to pull permits and such for blocking off streets, catering trucks, parking trailers, and running electrical cables, etcetera. We need to establish a shooting calendar based on the activities happening here in town, so I'll need an official list of times and a schedule."

Bailey would normally have done these things weeks before filming began, but she was in a pinch. "I apologize for hitting you with this all so last minute, but that's what we're dealing with—a last-minute save—so I appreciate it."

"I'll help with the permits. Leave me a list of all the specifics you need. Check with Miss Maureen at Evangeline House when you inquire about rooms there. She's still in charge of the Christmas Committee. She knows it all like clockwork. Nothing happens here without her blessing."

Bailey would need to make a list to send to the buyer ahead of time of anything else the set dressers required for filming. She would call Miss Maureen in the morning to see about stopping by for a meeting. Bailey had fond memories of Maureen Laroux, who was Cammie and Ben's mom. Bailey had spent quite a lot of time in their household over the years.

Speaking of Christmas magic... Seth had been a big part of Bailey's Christmas magic. Always. He'd not only been her boyfriend in high school, but they'd grown up together as neighbors outside of town. She couldn't remember a time that Seth wasn't nearby. He was tied to everything in Ministry. That's why coming back here wasn't as simple as avoiding Seth. That would have been easy. Avoiding memories of Seth was hard.

As she thanked him for his help, Bailey tried to distance herself from that tug toward him. She'd been back here an hour and it had already started. *Who do you think you are coming back here and pretending this is going to be easy because you're all grown-up and fancy?* Her inner child mocked her. How dare she get above her raising? Ugh. Her Alabama was showing already.

⫸⫷

AS BAILEY CROSSED the street to Mrs. Wiggins's house, she reset her resolve. She must not get dragged backward into the vortex of the past. Twelve years had passed since she'd left. Twelve years ago, Bailey tore herself away from everyone she'd ever loved to forge a new future. Coming back for more than a quick weekend was certainly risky, she'd known that. But this reaction at coming face-to-face with Seth?

If she'd looked into a crystal ball and seen, no *felt*, her reaction to Seth, Bailey might have tried harder to find a different little Christmas paradise—far from Alabama. Surely there were other places where perfect Christmases were guaranteed.

But Bailey knew everyone here; and they knew her. Time was short to get things done, and dealing with strangers would've been much harder. That's what she kept telling herself anyway.

As she rang the doorbell to Mrs. Wiggins's home, Bailey realized she was being watched. From the transom windows on either side of the massive front door stared sightless eyes about a foot from the ground. Bailey noticed the cats were staring at her but weren't moving, even after she'd rung the bell and knocked on the big door with the giant wreath and red bow.

The cats were real, clearly they were. How bizarre this was.

Mrs. Wiggins opened the door a small crack and inquired what her business might be.

"Hi there. I'm Bailey Boone. Sheriff McKay suggested I ask about vacancies. I'm looking to rent some rooms as soon as possible." Bailey couldn't help but notice how tiny Mrs. Wiggins really was. Smaller even than she remembered. Bailey wasn't super tall, but the woman couldn't be five feet even.

And those cats.

She continued to size Bailey up for another moment through the crack in the door. "Well, dear, if the sheriff sent you, I guess you'd better come on in." She opened the door wider. Wide enough for Bailey to get a gander at the sentinel cats. They were stuffed. Like by a professional. Real cats stuffed like when hunters killed wild game. And there were doilies. So many doilies and Tiffany lamps. She'd taken a step into the past.

"I saw you admiring my babies," she said.

Bailey stared at Mrs. Wiggins. She now questioned the woman's sanity. "Um, yes. They're—"

"Junior over at the taxidermist's office preserves my babies for perpetuity so I can always have them by my side," she said by way of explanation.

"O-oh. I've never heard of doing that with cats," Bailey said, working not to pass judgment of this strangeness.

The woman giggled. "That's alright. Some people think it's pretty weird but I don't give a dog's behind about their opinions."

She then noticed the delicious aroma. "Are you baking something?" Bailey couldn't help but ask.

"Why yes, dear. It's my shortbread. The coffee shop across the street sells it, so I pretty much bake it every day. Have been for years. You'll have to get used to it if you're going to stay here."

Bailey came out of her aromatic trance as her stomach growled loudly. "Oh, sorry. I just got into town. I haven't eaten lunch yet."

"Come into the kitchen and we'll talk turkey. Turkey sandwiches, that is." Mrs. Wiggins's shoes squeaked as she walked—or waddled more like. The woman was as sweet and kind as she'd barely remembered.

"Oh, you don't have to do that," Bailey protested.

"Honey, I'll never let it be said that I didn't feed a hungry traveler. Or one of my tenants. So, tell me about your need of my rooms."

The kitchen had been updated within the decade, thankfully, and Mrs. Wiggins constructed the most amazing sandwich—with piles of sliced turkey, honey mustard, fresh tomatoes, and tiny slices of red onions—Bailey had ever eaten. She wanted to cry with joy from the pleasure. Then the tiny woman added one thick slice of shortbread onto her plate, still hot from the oven.

"I've heard about the movie madness coming to our town in a matter of days. I'm assuming you'll need a place to stay for yourself and a few others?" she asked as Bailey continued to stuff her mouth and chew.

Bailey nodded and finally replied. "Yes. I would love to stay here, along with a few other people. I will let you meet them before they move in." Bailey figured if the coffee shop bought Mrs. Wiggins's food to sell and Bailey could see her way past the stuffed cats, this place was really pretty cool.

"I trust the sheriff. If he trusts you, then that's alright with me. How long will you need the rooms?" She snapped her tiny finger. "Wait a dang minute. You and the sheriff used to be an item when y'all were youngsters if I remember correctly. Well, that makes sense now." Mrs. Wiggins grinned slyly, as if she'd solved a great puzzle.

"Uh, yes. We, um, were kids back then. Only acquaintances now though," Bailey hurried to mitigate any early gossip. "Oh, until just before Christmas should be enough time for our principal actors to do their scenes on the set here in Ministry."

"Okay. I'll get to work on the leases. I keep the apartments move-in ready if you'd like to have a look now," she said with a weirdly shrewd sparkle in her eye.

Bailey had finally finished scarfing down her sandwich and was savoring the last crumb of shortbread. "Oh, okay. Sure. I figured I'd stay the night at my dad's or the inn tonight until I figured something out for myself."

Mrs. Wiggins squeaked over to a kitchen cabinet where there were several sets of keys hanging on cup holders. She pulled off the keys hanging on 1A and motioned for Bailey to follow her.

They climbed the stairs very slowly. She was again amazed by the doilies. Daddy had doilies that had been crocheted by Bailey's grandmother, the one she'd never met, in a trunk.

Mrs. Wiggins turned the key in the heavy door at the end of the hallway marked 1A. It was amazing. The ceilings were easily fourteen feet high. The floors were darkly stained wood and appeared to be freshly finished. The apartment smelled of beeswax and lavender. And the windows. They ran the length of the main living space and overlooked the charming downtown all decorated for Christmas. Bailey could see the Ministry Inn, the Pizza Pie, and the sheriff's office from her living room window.

The kitchen was small but efficient and updated. There was one bedroom and one bathroom. The place was tastefully decorated and had a good-sized flat-screen TV. "This is amazing," Bailey said, and truly meant it. "I can't believe these aren't rented all the time."

Mrs. Wiggins laughed. "I only rent when I want to whom I want."

"Well, I'll take it. How much is the rent?" Bailey asked.

"Seven hundred for the month, includes utilities. You'll have to bring your own trash down and drop it in the can out back. Trash day is Tuesday."

Seven hundred? "Are you sure that's all you're asking?" Bailey had to ask.

"Of course. This house has been paid for for years. I won't be accused of trying to overcharge anyone." Mrs. Wiggins appeared slightly miffed.

"Yes, but I don't think you're charging enough," Bailey said.

"Nonsense. We're not in California, you know," Mrs. Wiggins lifted her eyebrows in a knowing way.

Got it. "Thank you for allowing me to live in your lovely

home," Bailey said.

"So, you'll stay here tonight?" she asked. "There are sheets on the bed and linens in the drawer."

It was indeed move-in ready. The place was fully furnished. Even the kitchen had pots and pans ready for use. "You bet. I'll finish my errands and see you back here this evening."

"We can sign documents later. Here's the key. It opens the side door that leads to the tenants' staircase. I'll give you my phone number if you need anything," Mrs. Wiggins said. "Oh, and why don't you leave your suitcase here? Looks like you've been dragging it all over town today."

Had the woman been watching her roll her carry-on through town? Bailey looked down at her now-dusty luggage. She'd brought it with her because she'd believed there was a good possibility of ending up at the inn for the night. Funny how her day had meandered to this gorgeous place.

"I believe I will leave it here if you don't mind."

"Feel free to take a few minutes to freshen up." Mrs. Wiggins smiled sweetly as she said it, but Bailey wondered if she had something in her teeth.

"I will, thanks."

A good tooth brushing was exactly what she needed, since her day began back in L.A more hours ago than she could count. And maybe her hair could use a quick brushing. And lipstick wouldn't hurt.

Bailey waved as she crossed back to the other side of the

street. Well, that had been productive. Now, she had to do the other thing she'd been dreading. Dreading and not dreading. Seeing her daddy was the happy part.

Her heart beat faster just thinking about the drive out of town.

"Are you planning to drive out to your daddy's place in that?" Seth appeared in front of her as she made her way toward the side lot.

"In what?"

He nodded toward the perfectly capable compact economy rental.

"What? It's fine."

"Your daddy's road. That's what. That thing will rattle your teeth loose and leave parts scattered along the way, in case you've been gone so long you don't remember."

Bailey rolled her eyes, hating how right he was. She hadn't taken the extra insurance out on the car either. "I forgot about the gravel road when I leased it."

"I've got an idea. Why don't you take my Jeep Wrangler? I drive my sheriff's SUV wherever I go, but my Jeep sits behind the station most of the time unless I leave town for personal travel."

Bailey frowned. She didn't want to owe him. But she also didn't want to end up Flintstone-footing it back to town tonight in the tin can she'd rented. "Are you sure?"

He rolled his eyes at her this time. "I don't make offers unless I'm sure."

"Thanks for this. I'll try to upgrade this one tomorrow," Bailey said as he led her back toward downtown and the sheriff's office.

"I don't need the Jeep, and if I do, I'll let you know, so there's no sense in you paying to upgrade the rental. That would be a waste of someone's money."

Bailey agreed that it would. And right now, the budget was nonexistent when it came to upgrades of any kind. "I'll owe you one," Bailey said, though she tried not to wince at those words.

"No, you won't. My offer doesn't come with strings." Seth was frowning now, as if she'd offended him.

Bailey felt the need to make small talk. "So, the town looks great. Just like I remember." Better, even, she thought.

He nodded. "Christmas is always nice around here." He still seemed a little grouchy.

Yes, it was. And she was here to capitalize on that, both personally and professionally, which caused a little guilty pang in her gut. "Brings back a lot of memories." Now, why had she gone and said *that*?

He turned and gave her the stone-cold blue stare. "Yes, it does."

"Have I done something to annoy you?" she finally asked.

He narrowed his eyes at her as if trying to decide how to answer that. They'd arrived at the back of the sheriff's office, which was pretty much deserted. His gray, four-door Jeep stood waiting for her. He motioned for her to sit on the set of concrete steps that led to the back door of the sheriff's station.

"Bailey, I'm not annoyed with you, okay? I'm just trying to catch up," he said. "And we need to get something straight." They were sitting shoulder to shoulder on the top step. This was the closest Bailey had been to Seth McKay in twelve years, and she could feel his body heat sliding from him toward her. She could smell the aftershave or deodorant, or whatever it was that was the same as it had been over a decade ago.

And Bailey could almost physically feel his agitation. Not anger, exactly.

She cocked up an eyebrow in question. "Catch up?"

"With you. You have a lot of energy, and you walk and talk fast. I'm happy to help in whatever way I can; in fact, I want to help, and I know we'll see each other a lot in the coming days, so let's get something straight: You don't owe me. You *won't* owe me. Understood?"

She blinked. That was a lot of words strung together aimed at shaming her just a little. "Um, okay. But I'm a thanker. I will thank you when you assist me. Aames always taught me to tell people when I appreciate someone's help. Are you good with that?" she asked, slightly miffed with his tiny lecture.

The side of his mouth quirked up, like it had since they'd been kids. She called it his side smile. "I'm good with that," he said. "Let's get you in this Jeep. It's not driven nearly enough, so I'm glad to see it get some use."

"It's a beautiful automobile," Bailey said. She could tell he'd put a lot of extra after-market accessories on the Jeep. Growing up here, she'd learned a lot about four-wheel-drive vehicles, since most families owned at least one to manage some of the rough terrain in the area. "It reminds me of the old Jeep you had in high school—just a little."

Bailey and Seth had driven up and down every dirt road in the county as teens in that old Jeep, the music turned up loud.

They were both quiet for a minute, then Seth said, "Yeah, those were great times."

Chapter Three

DRIVING TO HER daddy's place a few miles outside of Ministry didn't take long, but the last mile happened to be a rutted red dirt road, which precipitated the need for a tougher vehicle than the one she'd rented. Bailey silently thanked Seth yet again for the kindness in lending her his Jeep. The weather in recent weeks made all the difference in the last stretch of getting home.

Home. Funny how coming back here put that word in her head, whether she liked it or not. But it was her home. Back in L.A., she could ignore the fact that she was from a dot on the map in Alabama where SEC football reigned supreme from fall until Christmas, depending on how the Crimson Tide fared versus the War Eagles of Auburn. Where homemade casseroles were the currency of family pride, and *bless your heart* may be murmured sympathetically because one lost a family member or more likely muttered as a verbal eye roll.

As she turned onto red dirt road, Bailey gave up fighting the memories as they washed over her. Coming back here was like taking a risk with her soul and her sanity. Yes, that was a bit dramatic, even for someone who worked in the movie industry, but that's what it felt like. The loss of her mother when she was a little girl seemed to have planted the seed of insecurity that grew into something as massive as one of the giant redwoods in the northern part of the state where she now resided.

Bailey's momma had "gone to heaven" when she was barely six years old, or that's what she'd been told by all the well-meaning folks around her. She'd been old enough to remember her touch; her smile, cookies, and hair-curling. But too young to remember the exact sound of her voice or the smell of her perfume. Almost though.

The fork in the road brought her back to the present. Bailey veered right of the old oak that still bore the hand-lettered sign with the peeling paint that said, POSTED—NO TRESPASSING. If she'd gone left, it would have led her to the small lake and the cabins where all her camp memories lay.

She gritted her teeth as the Jeep's tire dropped deep into a rut in the road. "Aagh." Why didn't Daddy do something about this drive?

With that thought, the house came into view and her heart sped up. It was the same as she'd remembered, an oversized, two-story log cabin. A porch ran the length of her childhood home. Bailey was hit with nostalgia that rivaled being mortared with a load of buckshot from her daddy's 12 gauge. But in a good way.

Home. She was home. Bailey barely had time to allow

the overwhelming sensation to wash over her before Daddy appeared on the front porch, a huge grin on his face. God, how she'd missed him.

Bailey slid the Jeep into park and hopped out to greet him. But before she started toward the porch, a deep wail nearly had her running for cover. Two enormous paws slammed her shoulders and pushed her backward against the vehicle. Bailey stared into the soulful eyes and saggy jaws of a massive hound.

"Groucho, you get down there and mind your manners, boy." There was a high pitch whistle and the big guy unpinned her, but not without leaving pawprints on her jacket.

Bailey knew there was a new dog but hadn't expected one quite so monstrous or adorable. "Groucho, huh? Yeah, that fits." The black *eyebrows* against the hound's tan fur gave him an animated expression—even more so than normal.

"Come give your old dad a hug, why don't you?" Daddy had made it down the porch steps to her by then.

"Hey, Daddy." She hugged him tight, inhaling the scent of him. His neatly trimmed beard had some gray in it that matched his hair perfectly. He'd turned fifty-seven this year. He was still fit and youthful and continued to work, though he threatened to retire every time his job added more regulations and paperwork to his daily routine.

Aames Boone was an Alabama Wildlife and Fisheries Agent. He knew about the outdoors and all the animals. And hunting and fishing. So, that's what they'd done when things got rough within their four walls during her childhood. They'd headed to the lake or the woods. Bailey's education did not resemble that of her peers. She'd been able to outshoot, outfish, or outhunt anybody, male or female, in any nearby county. It wasn't that she'd wanted it to be that way; it simply was. Bailey was involved heavily in 4-H and the local agriculture club.

And she'd loved TV and movies. She watched them endlessly on their less-than-perfectly-clear picture tube television in the living room. That had been her refuge. That, and her imagination. Writing. Painting. She was a creative in a place where it wasn't exactly celebrated.

"Well, sorry about that. Groucho is still a pup even though he's as big as a full-grown bear." Daddy frowned down at the animal, who now sat dutifully at his feet. "He gets excited from time to time, but he's a good one."

"He's adorable," Bailey said. That set Groucho's tail to wagging. "Who's a good boy?" she asked. But Bailey remembered her training commands and reminded Groucho to stay even as she showed affection.

"I'm glad you're finally home. Heard you been stirring up trouble in town already," he said, but there was a grin on his face.

"As in, I stopped by the sheriff's office? Word does travel fast around here." He started to grab her bags and she placed a hand on his arm.

"I'll be staying at Mrs. Wiggins's place in town since I

need to be on site for work."

"*Hmmph.* I heard a rumor about that too. Well, I hoped I would get at least one night with you here before you moved to town."

"I promised her I'd stay there tonight and pick up the leases for all the rooms I'm renting for the crew. I'll spend time out here whenever I can. Maybe before everyone arrives. After filming starts, it might be harder to get away."

They entered the house, and Bailey was hit with another heavy wave of nostalgia and the scent of home-cooked food. She inhaled. "Smells heavenly. Red beans and rice with sausage?"

He ruffled her hair like she was back in grade school. "You got it."

"I try to avoid meat most days, but—"

"Avoid meat? Since when? Lord, I wondered when California was gonna get to you."

Bailey held up her hand. "You didn't let me finish," she said. "I know your sausage is wild-caught and organic all the way, so I'll definitely make an exception." If Bailey was honest, it was easy to maintain a diet with little meat where she lived. There were so many vegetarian and vegan options in L.A. But given her current options, red beans, rice, and deer sausage smelled and sounded perfect.

"Come on in here while I stir the pot. You can make the salad," he said.

Bailey nodded as they moved toward the kitchen. She

looked around as they walked through the house. The smiling photos of her and her dad far outnumbered any others. But there were a few of her momma. Those were precious.

The aroma hit Bailey squarely in the face when they entered the kitchen. Daddy didn't know much about little girl things but he knew how to cook. In fact, Bailey was surprised he hadn't remarried after she'd flown the coop. Ministry was kind of known for being woman heavy. As in, the town had a higher population of single women than men. And her daddy was a catch, as things went here in Ministry.

"So, how are things in L.A.?" he asked while adding a healthy dose of Creole seasoning to his simmering kidney beans.

Bailey pulled out a head of lettuce, a couple tomatoes, a cucumber, and a red onion from the fridge and brought them to the large island workspace, pulling up a barstool to do her salad crafting. "I mean, it's L.A. Things are humming along. Most people are going vegan and checking Twitter regularly to make sure they haven't done anything wrong." Bailey shrugged.

He grinned and shook his head. "I guess everybody has to 'do them,' right?"

She nearly dropped the knife. "Wow, that's some big progress, Daddy." Whenever she'd flown him to the city, he'd regularly poked fun at the differences between their two worlds.

"What? It's not like I don't have the internet, or Netflix, for that matter."

"You have Netflix out here?" Bailey wondered what variety of space aliens had come and replaced her father with this modern man. Had she noticed a new flat-screen television when they'd gone through the family room that had been the home of a twenty-five-year-old dinosaur picture tube set he'd bought when she'd turned five?

"You act like I don't know what's happening in the world, but I do, or at least now I do."

Bailey narrowed her eyes. "Why now?" she asked.

He shrugged and turned off the burner under the pot of beans. The rice cooker sat nearby, its light showing that it was no longer cooking, but keeping the rice warm and ready to serve. Daddy said nothing else about his newfound self-awareness.

"Salad's ready," Bailey announced. She went in search of dressing or makings for a simple vinaigrette. It was while she stood peering into his refrigerator she noticed some odd items: white wine, olives, and fancy cheese. Her father hated olives. And he only drank beer. And she'd never seen any cheese fancier than pepper jack. Bailey's radar beeped wildly but she held her tongue and pulled out a bottle of organic raspberry vinaigrette. Another oddity.

The oven timer beeped, and Daddy pulled out a cookie sheet with what was obviously bread. So much for her grain-brain good intentions. The garlic butter sizzled atop the crispy baguette. "Ah. That looks so good."

"Your favorite, honey."

Bailey's stomach growled loudly at that moment. "Okay, let's eat."

"Hello?" A female voice called as someone entered the house. "Have I missed dinner?"

Bailey vaguely recognized the voice as the woman appeared.

※※※

JOELLA MCKAY, BESIDES being Seth's momma, had always been special to Bailey. She'd stepped in when Bailey was a little girl and had desperately needed a soft touch. And now, she was here, obviously invited by Bailey's daddy to dinner on her first night home.

They were sitting at the dining room table, something Bailey had rarely done with her daddy. "Bailey, I'm thrilled you're here. Ever since we found out you were coming home, Aames has talked about nothing else."

Bailey smiled politely and answered, "I have a hard time believing that."

"Your coming home is a big deal to me; you should know that. I hate that you won't be staying here. I'm trying to declutter a little around here and do some updating of the house," Daddy said.

When had the word declutter entered his vocabulary?

Then it clicked. He and Joella were dating. They were an item. *She* was the catalyst for the changes. White wine. Stinky cheese. Olives. Decluttering and Netflix.

Joella had been someone she'd really cared about throughout her childhood. It was odd now though, her sitting with them at the dinner table. After all, she was Seth's mother.

So far, Joella hadn't mentioned Seth. Maybe she was walking on eggshells, considering this was all uncharted territory. What were the odds of Bailey's dad and ex-boyfriend's mom becoming an item?

Probably better than normal due to the low number of single men like her father. And he and Joella had known one another forever.

Seth *was* an issue for Bailey, so maybe Joella wasn't mentioning him to tread lightly there. Seeing him today had rattled her even though she'd hoped it wouldn't, and she'd tried to prepare for it. If their parents were getting serious, it meant more exposure to Seth for Bailey. Something she'd intentionally avoided for a long time.

Bailey wanted to believe she was beyond their shared past. That he no longer mattered. But he'd been part of the tapestry of her childhood and teen years. The years and their mutual experiences had woven them together. Being back here meant he was unavoidable, even if she never saw his face in person. Everywhere she looked, he was there.

Now, he was figuratively sitting across the dinner table,

via Joella, his mom.

Might as well get this over with. "So, how long have the two of you been dating?" Bailey asked, trying for a smile and an upbeat tone.

Instead of appearing guilty, Daddy grinned and reached for Joella's hand, and she blushed like a young girl. "A few months now. I've been wanting to tell you, but it worked out better to tell you in person."

Joella laughed. "Well, Aames, you didn't *tell* her, did you? You kind of let her figure it out by herself."

"I should have been a little quicker on the uptake. The place is spotless and there's white wine and olives in the fridge." Bailey relaxed a little. "Dead giveaways in my book."

"I hope you're okay with this." Joella's gaze was questioning.

"It's clear that you're making him happy. Of course I don't mind. In fact, I'm happy for you both." Bailey said it, and she meant it—mostly.

Daddy let out a pent-up breath. "Thanks, baby."

"How's Seth taking it?" Bailey asked because she truly wondered what his reaction might be.

"He's getting used to the idea," Joella said, but sounded slightly uncomfortable with the topic.

"So, he's not okay with it?" Bailey asked.

"Not against it, maybe slightly skeptical. You know how he can be."

Yes, she knew how stubborn and overprotective he could

be. Especially with his mother. And with Bailey. "Yes. I do."

"You'll have to stop by the Pizza Pie. Anytime. And make sure you send some of those Hollywood folks in for a slice. That would be great for business." She changed the subject from Seth. No wonder she hadn't mentioned him right away. Joella was avoiding the topic.

Bailey nodded. "Sure thing." The Pizza Pie would likely be a hit with everyone from the studio. They usually liked sampling foods wherever they went. And Bailey could say for sure that the pizza was excellent.

Daddy cleared his throat and asked, "Do you think you might want to go through the stuff from your childhood up in the attic while you're here?" He pointed upward. "And your momma's things too. I thought you might want to have a look through them, honey."

Bailey stared at him as if the aliens had brought him back after replacing him with one of their own. He'd *never* offered her anything of her mother's. Never even mentioned that there was anything left. Bailey hadn't known Momma had anything in this house.

"Momma's things are in the attic?" she asked, her tone hollow.

"Well, sure they are, Bailey Bean. I kept them for you. When you were younger, it never seemed like a good time."

"I don't remember your offering," she said, trying not to sound accusing.

Daddy frowned and ran a hand through his hair. "I gotta

be honest, I don't remember if I ever did. I struggled for a long time after she passed, honey. I know that made it harder on you."

"And *now* you're telling me her things are up there, waiting for me to go through like it's no big deal?" Bailey fought tears. Her mother's death was the single most impactful thing besides leaving Seth that Bailey had endured. It had defined her.

"Oh, sweetie." Bailey noticed Joella reaching out a hand to her across the table. Part of Bailey wanted to take it— needed the comfort she offered. But she couldn't. This was between Daddy and her.

Bailey stood from the table. "I'll leave the two of you to enjoy your Netflix. I've got a lot to do tomorrow." She picked up her plate, carried it into the kitchen, and rinsed it out in the sink as the tears welled in her eyes. How does a thirty-year-old woman still cry over her momma who'd died when she was six?

Chapter Four

S ETH HAD TO admit he'd hung around the office longer
than normal hoping to catch Bailey as she returned to
Mrs. Wiggins's place for the evening. Word had it that
they'd struck a deal for lodging. *Word* being that Mrs.
Wiggins herself had squeaked over in her black orthopedic
shoes and given him the lowdown. The lovely woman was a
wellspring of information regarding the happenings in
Ministry.

"She's grown into a real beauty, hasn't she now?" Mrs.
Wiggins asked, referring to Bailey, but continued before he
could respond, "They've rented the entire place until a few
days before Christmas. I mean, can you believe they can
shoot a whole movie in under a month's time?"

Seth listened and made the appropriate nods and noises.
"I don't think they have a whole movie to shoot, just the
outdoor scenes. Their other location fell through about
halfway into filming."

Mrs. Wiggins nodded, as if she'd learned something essential. "Thanks for keeping me posted, Mrs. W. It's always
good to know what's going on around town. I'll catch up

with Bailey later."

"Oh, I imagine the two of you will have a lot to talk about while she's here." Mrs. Wiggins clapped her tiny hands together. "I can't wait to see how this all shakes out. You know I've seen your momma and her daddy together around town lately. Joella appears as happy as I've ever seen her since your poor daddy passed, God rest his soul."

Seth tried hard not to roll his eyes. "Thanks for bringing the news about Bailey and the movie folks, Mrs. Wiggins. I've got some work to do before I leave for the day, so—"

She grinned. "Alright, my boy, we won't discuss your momma. I've got baking yet to do and I'm finishing up the lease paperwork for Bailey. I'll see you soon." She winked at him and exited the office.

Cheryl, from over on the police department side of the office, snickered.

"Not a word, Cheryl."

She'd ignored his command. "Oh, come on, Sheriff. You're gonna have to come around about your momma and Aames Boone. He's a good citizen, despite the fact that he's Bailey's daddy."

He gave her a hard stare. "She's my mother."

Cheryl relented. "Okay, okay. I'm just sayin', you don't get to pick who she spends her time with. And she could do a lot worse."

He knew that was true. Aames Boone *was* a good person and his character couldn't be questioned. And he and Aames were friends. But seeing his momma around town, out to dinner, on dates with him didn't sit well. Yes, Seth wanted her to be happy. Of course he did. It simply made Seth grumpy to watch her behaving like a giddy teen with Aames.

Now, as Seth waited for Bailey, Cheryl was long gone for the day. The lights were on in Mrs. Wiggins's house across the street. From his desk, he could easily see the entrances to her home. If he were paying attention, there was no way Bailey could approach without him noticing. No, he wasn't being creepy. He just wanted to make certain she made it home safely.

Seth knew she'd gone to Aames's house for dinner because he'd been notified of the plan by his mother earlier in the day. It wasn't his fault that he was apprised of her movements. He understood that might sound a little creepy so he'd need to not go out of his way to keep tabs on her.

But she was back. It gave him such an amazing feeling of relief to know she was out of harm's way from the big city, if only for the time she was here. Knowing she wasn't out someplace in California alone, walking in the dark, putting herself at risk did something to relieve the low-level anxiety he'd carried for her since Bailey had left Alabama.

That's how much he'd worried for her, thought about her over the years. Maybe it was too much; not his business, for sure. The thinking of her, and the concern about her. Seth understood he wasn't the person Bailey intended to spend her life with, but he couldn't help the way he felt about her. Still.

And surely they could talk to each other without it being too weird. He would like that. At least they could be friends since they'd be forced to work out the movie schedule details together. Both were adults now, right?

He spotted Bailey moving from a parking spot in front of the inn toward Mrs. Wiggins's house across the street. She had a duffel bag and her purse slung over her shoulder. He imagined she'd had a long day since flying in from L.A. with a connection in Atlanta, then to Huntsville, with an hour-and-a-half drive from there.

Seth quickly locked up the office and hurried across the street. He caught up with her as she rang Mrs. Wiggins's doorbell. It was barely seven thirty, so not too late that she'd wake the woman.

"Hey there. I was hoping to catch you," he said from behind her.

By the way she jumped, and stifled a scream, Bailey plainly wasn't expecting him to appear out of nowhere in the dark, even though the lanterns lit the streets pretty well. "You scared me half to death. Are you stalking me?" She didn't seem pleased to see him.

"No, sorry. I was working late and saw you. I thought I would say hi and make sure everything went okay on your first day back."

"I'm fine. Just tired."

"I apologize for scaring you." Seth realized then that she

lived in L.A., and she had every right to jump when a man approached her in the dark.

⟫⟪

SETH APPEARED SINCERE. But his showing up right as she was ringing the doorbell did seem slightly shady.

Mrs. Wiggins opened the door then. "Oh, hi, kids. Come on in."

The creepy cats stood sentinel. She would have to get used to that.

"Hi there. I hope I'm not showing up too late," Bailey apologized. She knew older people often went to bed early.

"Honey, I just took out the last batch of shortbread. No early to bed for this old gal."

They laughed.

Seth came right on in with Bailey. "Hello again, Sheriff."

"Hi, Mrs. Wiggins. I wanted to check in with Bailey. I imagine she's had a long day."

Bailey *had* had a long day. In fact, all she wanted was to collapse in the clawfoot tub upstairs up to her neck in scented bubbles. It's what she'd been thinking about nonstop for the last hour or so.

"Yes, I'm exhausted. Thanks for checking on me, but I'm good, as you can see. I guess I'll see you tomorrow and we can discuss some details about getting the Christmas schedule ironed out." That was pretty loud and clear.

"Here, Sheriff, you can carry Bailey's suitcase upstairs for her." Mrs. Wiggins motioned toward her carry-on that she'd left there earlier.

Bailey relied again on her acting skills to not stomp her foot like a child at being thwarted out of her immediate bubble bath. "Thanks." Her smile probably wouldn't win her an Oscar.

Seth grinned and grabbed the handle. "Lead the way," he said.

The last thing Bailey wanted was Seth in her private area where she slept. But it would sound silly to protest his help. So they climbed the ancient staircase, and Mrs. Wiggins led them down the hall from the apartment she'd used to freshen up in earlier. She unlocked the door to the lovely apartment. It smelled like roses and beeswax simultaneously. "I decided to put you in the same unit that my sweet former tenant Rachel, the town photographer, lived in before she married. There are such great vibes in here."

"It's lovely," Bailey said. And it was, with more feminine furnishings and draperies than the other one she'd seen earlier in the day. "It's perfect. Thank you."

"I'll leave this in the bedroom." Seth started toward what was obviously the bedroom.

"No. Leave it here," she might have said a little too force-fully.

"Oh. Okay. Sure." He released the handle of the suitcase but looked her in the eye as he did so. Something passed between the two of them, and she experienced a slight electrical sensation throughout her body. It was something familiar from a time long past.

Seth moved to the window instead of the door leading outside, his big, man-body taking up space in her apartment. "Wow, what a view of the town you've got from here, Bailey. You can wave at me while I'm in my office anytime." He grinned, those white, straight teeth still so appealing.

"Remind me to keep my curtains drawn," she replied, half-joking.

"I was kidding." He might not have been kidding.

"I need to go check on my shortbread now," Mrs. Wiggins interrupted their banter. "Bailey, I left the lease paperwork on the kitchen table. There's a spare key to the side entrance as well, but feel free to use the front door anytime you see the lights on. Good night, all."

"Thanks so much," Bailey said. "I'll drop the documents by tomorrow."

Seth didn't walk out with Mrs. W as she'd expected.

"I'm pretty tired, so—" she hinted yet again.

He sighed. "I know you're trying to get rid of me. And I know I make you uncomfortable. I wanted the opportunity to tell you again how glad I am that you're home—even if it's only for a few weeks. The town's never been the same since you left."

Bailey felt the familiar heart tug at his confession. The one she'd avoided by staying away from Alabama. "Thanks, Seth. That's kind of you to say. It should be fun being back for a little while. I've missed Daddy so much. And I was surprised to see Joella at dinner tonight."

That should back him off a little, seeing how this was a topic he didn't approve of, based on what she'd learned earlier this evening.

He frowned. "Uh, yeah. I guess you saw they're all lovey-dovey, huh?"

"Yes. My daddy had white wine in his refrigerator. It was a clear sign something was up."

"I guess they could both do worse," he said and shrugged.

They were standing in her tiny kitchen, where he seemed to take up a great deal more space than he should.

"They definitely could. Especially with the casserole brigade around here. I vaguely remember when my momma died how many women brought casseroles and how Daddy had to politely call the phone number taped to the bottom of the dishes and thank them after we ate the food. I learned years later they were the single women trying to lure him with their best dish, or so the story went."

"The casserole brigade is definitely still a thing. I sprained my ankle a few years ago and was inundated with them. I didn't get to a few of the dishes and forgot to call with the proper thanks. Let me tell you, I heard about my rudeness afterward." His shoulders relaxed and he became animated as he told his tale. This was how she remembered him. Talkative and funny.

Bailey laughed despite herself. "Oh, I can see it now. What a lame excuse to come at you." The idea that the single women in town had descended on Seth due to a sprained ankle tickled her.

"It doesn't take much. I'm hoping that online dating will catch on here as a means for options. There's nothing wrong with meeting someone in a town or two over," Seth said.

"It's a shame they don't go elsewhere and find lives and happiness instead of being so competitive and vulturish here in this town. Women should and can do better," Bailey said. This was one reason she liked living in a bigger city. The idea of competing with other women for a few men sounded sad.

"I agree. I just think they are so used to thinking the same as their mothers' generation. It's like we're twenty or so years behind here in some ways."

Gosh, how had they gone this far on a tangent? Time to redirect or she'd never get him out of here. "Okay, back to my having a long day," she said and shook her head, smiling. It had always been like this with them. They'd been involved romantically, but still were friends who could talk about things—anything—for hours.

"I'm leaving. But it's been great seeing you, Bailey." He flashed her that million-dollar smile again. The female director would want him in the close-up crowd scenes once she got a look at him. "I promise not to stalk you. Obviously we've got movie stuff to talk about starting tomorrow morning, but besides that, this is Ministry and things are bound to come up, so call me anytime."

They both understood the odd characters and happenings around their tiny hometown. Bailey nodded and opened the door for Seth. "No doubt. Thanks for your help with housing ideas for the cast and crew. This is a great place to stay while I'm in town."

"Anytime." He nodded as he removed himself from her apartment. She could still smell his aftershave. How could he smell so good this many hours after he'd applied it?

As his boots thumped down the stairs, Bailey decided that maybe she'd need to try a little harder to defend herself against Seth McKay's charms.

>>>>><<<<<

SETH MADE HIS way in the low light of the downtown's snazzy new lanterns toward the front of his office. His four-wheel-drive SUV with large tires was equipped to handle any terrain or weather that he might need to navigate the backwoods of rural Alabama. It bore the seal of the sheriff's department emblazoned on both sides, back and front. Seth drove it proudly because it meant he'd earned the trust of the people in Ookaloosa County. But he didn't have to climb inside to drive home. He was home.

Upstairs was a loft almost as large and fine as Bailey's apartment at Mrs. Wiggins's house. The city and county had worked together and created a living space above the office for the local sheriff or the chief of police, should either require lodging during their tenure.

Cheryl was married and lived less than a mile from town, so Seth had moved upstairs for the convenience since he'd lived on the ranch with his momma after his daddy passed to help with the workload. She'd recently sold the horses and the property and moved into a lovely home that required less maintenance.

Everything Seth did either on duty or off was up for public scrutiny. And for gossip of course. He hadn't lived his thirty years here not to understand that. So, he'd need to take care when it came to how he handled things with the whole movie circus coming to town. Bailey was the ringleader for all the chaos about to descend, and he'd need to keep his head on straight no matter how he felt about her.

When they'd been kids and their daddies had been fishing buddies, their fathers had taken the two of them along in the boat and let them play together, fish together, and swim together. They'd been as close as siblings. Joella would have supper waiting for them, or if enough legal-sized fish were caught that day, she would fry them up outside with hush puppies and they would chase lightning bugs until the mosquitoes got too bad.

Bailey had been a tomboy and tough as nails—always. Seth respected that about her. She'd never whined about getting a splinter when they climbed trees or picked blackberries out behind her house. Maybe because she didn't have a mother to teach her how to be more girlish when she was young.

Seth understood how much Bailey had missed her momma after she died. She'd even cried about it sometimes, which had made him uncomfortable, though he'd tried not to show it.

Tonight, they'd had a simple conversation, and for a precious few minutes, the years fell away and it was almost like before. Back when they could debate or discuss something without all the years of baggage.

She smelled the same too. Seth always loved how she smelled. Fresh, like she'd been out in the woods picking flowers. But he guessed she didn't get to do that often in L.A. And *that* was a crying shame considering how much time she'd spent doing it throughout her childhood.

Chapter Five

BAILEY'S PHONE ALARM shrieked its usual awful noise. But it took her a minute to recognize the sound. Her first impulse was to fling the offending thing across the room a second before she realized the reason it sounded different today. Today it had woken her up. It never woke her up. Every other day, she'd set it as an unlikely precaution. Because she *never* slept until her alarm.

Today, Bailey willed her eyelids to open and stay that way while the terrible sound continued. Her brain finally caught up with what was happening enough to tell her hand to reach out a finger to the touch screen to shut that infernal racket off. She rubbed her eyes and tried to remember going to bed last night. Bailey looked around the room with bleary eyes. *Oh, yeah.* She really was back in Alabama. But she'd slept like the dead. Which never happened. Like, *never.*

It was quiet here in this old house overlooking the downtown of Ministry. L.A. wasn't quiet, even in the dead of night. As soon as Bailey had been financially able, she'd moved to the city from Highland Park, where she'd initially had to share a one-bedroom apartment with two hopeful girls in the early stages of their acting careers. They'd met in college. Different paths, same industry.

But sleep wasn't the thing that drew Bailey to the city, obviously. That was something she'd given up ages ago. The ability to get to work at the studio without having to spend a ridiculous amount of time in traffic every day made it worth every cent. Well, almost.

For a moment, when the realization hit that she'd gotten at least eight, unheard-of, uninterrupted hours of dead-to-the-world sleep, Bailey wondered if she'd gotten her priorities wrong. As she sat up in bed, and stretched better than she ever had in yoga, then yawned hugely, Bailey decided this night's sleep was one of the best gifts she'd gotten in years. But she would keep that to herself. Should anyone find out she had something good to say about being home, they would hit her over the head with a great big, *I told you so*.

And that was something Bailey avoided whenever possible.

The heavenly smell of Mrs. Wiggins's shortbread suddenly permeated her brain, but her glow of sleep excellence and sensory delight was harshly interrupted by the shrill sound of her phone ringing. The familiar number popped up on her phone as it did many mornings.

Bailey put the boss's assistant, Jem, on speaker as she went in search of a Keurig. Jem could be a giant pain but also a necessary one to Bailey's job. "Yes, Jem, I've arrived and am in the process of getting accommodations for everyone. I should know in a couple days about the talent trailers. I have to speak to the sheriff about the space available for them and the honey wagon." The honey wagon housed the bathrooms, so required a way to run the sewerage, and it held small rooms for day players and stunt players while they were filming. There would be a hair and makeup trailer and a wardrobe trailer, not to mention producer, director, and teamster trailers. There were others as well, but right now, Bailey would take things a step at a time. She had a feeling there would be some improvisation necessary. She would know more after she met with Seth.

The mere mention of Sheriff McKay brought to mind the mental picture of the grown-up Seth. And how he filled out his Wranglers. *Yes, she'd noticed he still wore the same brand as when he was nineteen.* They were utterly timeless in her opinion.

Bailey rooted around in the kitchen but didn't see a coffeepot. Not one from this decade. There was one, but it required knowledge from her childhood that she no longer possessed. As she eased Jem's mind about the trailer space, she made a mental note to have Keurigs placed in all the rooms for the talent. There were levels of items that were required depending on the person's title. Assistants got no Keurigs. They would either have to figure out how to use the antiquated coffeepots or wait until they got on set for coffee.

It was a matter of the budget. If it were up to Bailey, everyone would be treated the same. But it wasn't and they weren't, so she would order what she couldn't buy here in town. Hopefully, rural delivery would be within a reasonable window.

"Wait, why do you need to speak to the sheriff about the trailers? How far out in the sticks were you raised?"

She ignored that. "He's currently the point person here in town," Bailey said, hoping it would be a satisfactory explanation, while she slipped her sensible Chuck Taylors on. No sense in being laughed out of town by wearing something the locals would consider ridiculous. And she certainly wouldn't want to be accused of "*big-timing*" them by wearing expensive brands and showing off. Of course, these items would be normal, everyday non-head turners where she lived. But there was no quicker way to have her efforts at cooperation around here fail at every turn.

"Oh my. Your hometown is like an episode of *Schitt's Creek*," Jem said, referring to a popular show streaming on Netflix. Bailey could hear the horror/amusement in her voice. She and Jem were friends—sort of. Jem worked for the boss, Jeremy Stone. And when push came to shove, Jem was the arm of the boss.

"I guess that's a good recent comparable. I would've spoken to the mayor about all this but he's out of town." Honestly, the town reminded Bailey more of those old reruns of Andy Griffith set in Mayberry RFD, which nobody in her generation had ever seen or heard of. Daddy used to watch them all the time when she was a little girl. For some reason she'd loved them. There was a sheriff with a little motherless boy whom Bailey had identified with painfully.

Jem laughed outright over her last comment. Jem would no doubt share this information with everyone in the office. Nothing was more amusing to city folk than backwoods country folk.

"Careful where you step. And let me know when you get all the accommodations worked out." Jem hung up still laughing at her own joke about stepping in cow manure.

So funny. But not as unlikely as one might think.

Bailey shook it off. Jem's attitude wasn't so different than her own with regard to this town during all the years she'd been away. She'd made her share of cracks about her hometown in Alabama. But hearing someone else make fun of it in a slightly nasty way annoyed her.

Bailey guessed it was like poking fun at your own family; all was fair game until someone on the outside piped up, then everybody came together to take them down. Or so she'd heard. Well, she'd watched a lot of movies and television. Growing up with no mother and no siblings hadn't given her much sense of what that might be like. Her grandparents were long gone. She still had an aunt someplace in Atlanta. But Bailey was very protective of her daddy. Maybe that's why she had a little hesitation when it came to his letting someone else in their very small circle. Heck, it wasn't even big enough to make a circle.

A text sounded on her phone, which brought her back to

the task at hand. Her coworker, Alexis, was flying in today and would arrive around three o'clock. Bailey had needed this head start to make contact here in Ministry before her tiny, firecracker coworker arrived. They'd worked together in small towns several times, so Alexis, being the fast learner she was, understood that a different skill set was required here than in an urban location.

But it might behoove Bailey to remind her again before Alexis hit the ground running. The tiny but efficient woman spoke fast, moved with stealth, and was a problem solver who didn't take no for an answer. Which might not go over so well here. Here, everything was a negotiation.

So Bailey texted Alexis: *Keep in mind you're traveling to a slower-paced world. These are people I grew up with. Go easy...* ☺

Alexis: *Oh good Lord, Bailey. Glad I packed my Xanax.* ☹

Alexis would do fine. It might take a day or two, but she understood how to relate to people. It was her job and she loved her job as much as Bailey loved hers.

So far, Bailey had gotten ten of the fifty or so of the rooms for the next four weeks. She'd better get cracking. And she really could use three or four cups of coffee.

Bailey headed downstairs and knocked on Mrs. Wiggins's door, the aroma of shortbread now enveloping her. The diminutive woman answered the door holding a live feline that stared at her with pale yellow eyes that could quite possibly see into her soul.

"Well, good morning, Bailey Boone. I hope you slept well on your first night home." Mrs. Wiggins blinked up at her and opened the door wider as if she should enter.

"I actually did sleep well, thank you. I wanted to give you the paperwork and find out if I could get your electronic deposit information to make the rent payments."

Mrs. Wiggins frowned. "We don't do that here, dear. I take checks or cash. You can pay on the first of each month."

"Oh. Okay. I'll need to speak with my boss's production assistant and get a paper check overnighted."

"It's alright. I trust you, dear. I've got some coffee made. Let me pour you a cup."

Before Bailey could protest about not having time to stay and drink it, the woman had moved toward a percolator like the one in her room and snagged a cup off one of the tiny hooks that held one of many mugs.

"Oh. Thank you. I didn't take time to make any this morning."

"Cream? Sugar?" Before she could decline the heavy cream and real, white sugar, Mrs. W had spooned in two teaspoons of it and added at least a tablespoon of cream from her tiny crockery.

"Oh—sure."

It was pure heaven. Bailey tried to stay away from the real stuff, instead, ordering her skinny latte with almond milk. But—holy moly—was it worth the sacrifice all these years?

Before she could take a second sip, a tiny plate appeared in front of her with a single slice of shortbread. Weak. She was weak. And tried to use her best manners in not devouring the cookie in one bite.

Bailey used the proffered napkin to wipe her mouth. "This was such a treat. Thanks again for accommodating us. I'll bring the check to you as soon as I get it. I assume the post office is still in the same place?"

"Yes, it's still where it was. Where it has been for the last fifty years that I know of." The elderly woman smiled as if having Bailey in her kitchen was the best thing ever.

Bailey experienced a warm, cozy sensation at Mrs. Wiggins's kindness. "That's my next stop then. Thanks for breakfast."

"Have a nice day, dear," Mrs. Wiggins said, then she added, "Oh, and if you see my kitty, Scarlett O' Hara while you're out, would you see her home for me?"

"Oh, is she missing?" Bailey asked. "What does she look like?" She hadn't remembered seeing the live feline around.

"She's a large calico. You can't miss her."

"Okay, I'll keep an eye out."

"Thanks, Bailey. And do have a lovely day."

It was as if she had a grandmotherly angel wishing her well for the day after feeding her delicious sugary treats. And as much as she should feel guilty about drinking heavy cream and eating who knew how much butter and sugar in that one slice of shortbread, Bailey decided to simply appreciate the kindness and move forward.

She had brought her running shoes though. It might be a good idea to plan for more running if she was going to eat her weight in shortbread while she was here.

>>>«««

SETH HAD JUST returned from a call that consisted of a neighborly dispute right outside of town. Cows. Darn cows. They continued to break out of their fencing and poop on the neighbor's yard. It was a recurring problem.

Seth climbed out of the SUV and was deciding what to do about his boots. Change them or clean them? Cheryl would give him the devil of a hard time if he went in with them on as they presently were. They had an agreement: Don't stink the place up. No tuna sandwiches or cow manure on your boots; and a few other items not worth mentioning. It was a pretty simple verbal contract. He'd broken it more than once and decided the price was more than he wanted to pay currently. He appreciated Cheryl's honesty and friendship. She appreciated clean air. And he despised tuna; the mere whiff of it made him gag. So, unless he wanted to live with the stench of it for the next week as her lunch, the poop boots were an outside deal.

So embroiled in his current dilemma, he'd nearly missed Bailey crossing the street toward the post office. Ministry had been set up long ago for convenience. The original planners had laid things out like the old Western towns. The bank, post office, sheriff's department, inn, town bar, and various other businesses sat right along the main drag downtown. And off to the side was the town greenspace, or the square where folks congregated. It was where they put up the giant Christmas tree during the holidays and where fireworks were enjoyed on the Fourth of July and New Year's Eve. There was a large fountain in the center where coins were thrown and many wishes made.

So when Seth did spot Bailey out of the corner of his eye this time, he covertly lowered his focus back down to his boots as if he'd not noticed her. The last thing they needed was to get people in town talking. Because that was never a good thing.

And his surprising her when she arrived home last night wasn't exactly a smooth move.

Seth reached for his number two pair of boots in the back of his vehicle hoping he'd not already, well, gotten some number two on *them*. But they appeared alright. A little crusty, but nothing he couldn't knock off on the curb before heading inside. The current ones would require hosing off, so he carried them out back of the office and set to work.

As the hosing commenced, Cheryl came over the two-way on their dedicated channel. "Sheriff, we've got an out of towner making her way toward the Pizza Pie. Looks like a jaywalker to me. I'm a little busy right now with important city business. Thought you might want to cover me. Over."

Good ol' Cheryl. She had his back whether or not she liked to admit it. "Ten-four, Chief. I'll be there as soon as I finish rinsing off these offensive-smelling boots. Thank you for your efforts. Over."

City offenses might always be considered county offenses since they occurred inside the county lines. There were technicalities in every line of work. But the sheriff and the chief of police worked together to keep their citizens safe; that fact was undisputed here in Ministry and its surrounding areas.

BAILEY HAD A long list of people to talk to and things to cover today. She'd made mental lists to add to her physical ones, even as she'd relaxed in the most delightful tub of hot water and bubbles. One item she'd added to the list was to swing by the Pizza Pie for old times' sake and say hi to Joella.

Bailey really was happy about their budding relationship. Daddy was alone here and getting older. It relieved her that he had somebody. It had bothered her that he'd spent his days going to work in the woods or on the lake—alone.

So, before she got in the Jeep, Bailey decided to take a step back to the past, where she'd spent so much time during her formative years in Ministry.

The Pizza Pie had bells on the door, still, and they jingled *almost* pleasantly as she entered. The place hadn't changed as far as the vibe went. Its walls were still painted bright blue with neon slices of pizza adorning them, with other neon curly cues here and there. The upgrades were that it was clean as a whistle and had newly installed booths and tables.

Of course, it was also decorated for Christmas, like all the businesses and homes in Ministry. There were green, red, and blue lights strung all around, and wreaths hung on the front doors. It was still a super-groovy lunch spot, and the smell of Pizza Joe's incredible crust made Bailey's stomach growl.

"Good morning, Bailey. What a pleasant surprise." Joella came out from the back at the sound of the bells, she assumed. Joella wore a white apron with reddish-orange spots of what Bailey assumed was pizza sauce. Joella stood behind the counter that had been there for decades.

"Hi there. The place looks amazing, Joella. Brings back lots of memories." And it did. Most of them involved Seth, of course. The two of them as kids hanging out together in the summers sharing a milkshake with money they'd scrounged up between them while their parents were at work. When they weren't working at Camp Grandview on Bailey's family property. It truly did have a grand view.

"I imagine it does. You and Seth were in and out of here all the time, weren't you?" She grinned. "I knew I didn't need to look far to find him. Y'all were always joined at the hip."

Bailey tried to smile, but something about Joella's comment made her want to burst into tears, so she changed the subject. "I'm glad you and Daddy have found each other. It relieves my mind to know he's got you to look after him."

"Thanks, sweetie. It's great to have you back."

"I'm glad it's you instead of someone I've never met." *That would've been awful,* she admitted to herself.

"Honey, don't you worry. If things fall apart, it won't be anybody's doing but ours. We're grown people going into this with open eyes. And we're not after each other's money."

Another elephant in the room, maybe. "Thanks for your honesty, Joella. Daddy's all I've got; you know that."

"I've known you since you were born, Bailey. I knew your beautiful momma; we were friends and had babies and young children the same age. We were neighbors. I grieved when she died. You and Seth grew up almost as close as siblings. You've been dear to my heart all these years and still are. Keep your worry for something that requires it."

Joella removed her apron, then came from around the bar and pulled Bailey into a gentle but firm hug. The kind that people who loved you gave. Bailey nearly melted against her. It was rare that she allowed herself to receive affection. In L.A., people hugged and showed affection within the arts community, but Bailey hadn't become close enough to anyone during her time there for it to penetrate beyond the superficial.

This kind of tender affection was motherly and loving.

And so foreign to Bailey's life in the past many years that she'd not remembered the last time it had happened. In fact, maybe Joella had actually been the last person to embrace her like this. Her daddy, yes. Their hugs were filled with love. But no one else got so near. Not women.

❯❯❯❮❮❮

BAILEY HAD TO stop by Seth's office before heading out to Evangeline House and meet with Maureen Laroux about lodging for some of the talent. There were so many details when it came to setting up the base camp where the trailers and equipment would be stationed. She had several questions for Seth to mark off the list.

As she opened the door to leave the Pizza Pie, Bailey ran smack-dab into a shiny gold badge. And a man who smelled as good as she remembered. "Oh—it's you. I was just—"

"Coming to find me?" He grinned. "Cheryl said she saw you heading this way, and I thought I'd save you a trip." He held up a manila folder and then handed it to her. "Some of the things you asked for."

"Oh. Thanks. I'm about to head over to Evangeline House," Bailey said. They were walking toward the Jeep now.

"Mind if I join you? It wouldn't hurt to have me along as a goodwill ambassador."

Bailey raised her brows. "Is that necessary?" she asked.

"No. Probably not. But I'm fresh from an annoying cattle call, so it might do us both some good."

She eyeballed him in question.

He shook his head. "Don't ask."

They'd made their way to the Jeep. "Do you want to drive?" she asked and dangled the keys. After all, it was his Jeep.

"Nah. You go ahead. Do you remember how to get there?" he asked.

"Oh, come on. It's not like I don't have a permanent map of this town," Bailey laughed. "Who doesn't know where Evangeline House is that's been here more than once even?"

He shrugged his shoulders. His very wide shoulders. They'd both climbed up into the Jeep and he was taking up far too much room in the small space of the cab.

Chapter Six

THE DRIVE TO Evangeline House was like something out of a movie set. The town of Ministry prided itself on its historic homes and clean, crisp blocks and landscaped lawns. Obviously, December wasn't the prettiest time for lawns, but the residents here made up for less-than-green grass by adorning their homes with fabulous lights, wreaths, and yes, faux snow.

"I'd forgotten about the fake snow they put down at Christmas," Bailey said.

"A winter wonderland, one way or another," Seth said.

"Look at this place. It's like stepping into the past." It was the same as she'd pictured in her memory. Evangeline House was especially popular this time of year because it was the go-to spot for hosting holiday events both large and small. The enormous historic mansion and grounds was two acres plus of pure perfection.

Back when Bailey lived in Ministry, it was the home of Cammie Laroux and her four siblings, all older besides Ben, her twin brother. They all still lived here in town, which made Bailey wonder how they did it.

Bailey rang the doorbell after she and Seth climbed the twenty or so steps up the front porch. Everything here seemed massive. And impressive. No wonder Miss Maureen had decided to turn it into a bed-and-breakfast now that all her brood had homes of their own. It was an incredible home.

A man answered the door. "Well, hello there, Ms. Boone, and Sheriff McKay, and come on in. I'm Howard." He stuck out his hand. He was tall and wore starched denim jeans and a red and black plaid shirt. His gray hair was neatly combed and his manner polished and confident.

Bailey shook his hand. "Hi. I'm here to see Maureen Laroux."

"Hey, Howard. How's it going?"

"Having a good day, we are," Howard answered. "Let me go and get Maureen."

He led her inside beyond the high-ceilinged foyer into what might be termed a family area. The smell of pine was almost overwhelming. Fresh garland hung everywhere, accented with holly berries and white lights. There was a huge flat-screen TV and many lovely but comfortable couches and artfully arranged chairs and sofa tables. The seating pieces were mostly solids, with printed pillows and throws. The comfortable atmosphere would invite gatherings of all sorts from family football games to cozy functions. Bailey could see hosting a cast and crew party here.

She looked up when she heard her name. "Oh, hi, Bailey.

Sheriff. It's so lovely to see you again." Maureen Laroux descended the *Gone with the Wind*-like staircase with such grace and beauty she might have stepped right out of the movie itself. Bailey appreciated a grand entrance. Made extra grand by the insane amount of lit garland.

"Hi, Miss Maureen. I wasn't sure you'd recognize me. It's been several years since we've seen each other." Bailey suddenly reverted to the little girl and teen wondering if she was invisible to adults.

Miss Maureen folded her into a similar hug as Joella had, amidst a light cloud of Chanel No. 5 that mixed with the pine. Though the hug wasn't quite as familiar and didn't last nearly as long. "Of course I remember you, darling. You ran around here with Cammie nearly your whole life. But you were a shy one in a crowd if I recall." The woman tilted her head as if she was recollecting something specific. "You are a near carbon copy of your mother at this age; God rest her soul." She closed her eyes briefly as if taking a moment of prayerful respect for Bailey's dearly departed mother.

Bailey wasn't used to anyone referencing her mother, and now two women had done so in the span of an hour. When Bailey was a child, nobody discussed her, maybe for fear of upsetting either Daddy or her. "I—didn't realize that. Thank you for saying so," Bailey responded for lack of something better to say. The photos on the wall at home were as faded with time as her memory. The idea that she and her mother actually had things in common hadn't occurred to her.

"Oh, yes. She was a creative, you know. Always reading and writing when the muse struck. I'm assuming you are still a reader, and a writer too? Like you were as a child?" she asked.

If the woman had thrown a brick at her head, Bailey wouldn't have been more surprised by the words that came out of the genteel mouth. How could she even respond? How could Bailey say that she hadn't known these things about her own momma? Her mother had been a writer? Daddy never talked about Momma, so really, how would she know?

Standing there with her eyes bugging out and her mouth catching flies probably wasn't the professional adult persona Bailey was going for, so she pulled it together as best she could. Later. Later she would process the information she'd learned.

Seth leaned over and whispered, "You okay?"

Bailey nodded. She was suddenly glad he was there with her.

"I didn't realize you had such a sharp memory of me as a child. I hardly recall some of those things." But she did, mostly because of feeling different from other girls. Bailey's nose was often stuck in books to avoid the group activities. Writing wasn't a choice though. Her thoughts required an outlet. Bailey wrote story after story so no one could call her out for writing about them in a journal. Best to shroud her angst in fiction.

"I had lots of children running freely about, but I remember the interesting ones. And my favorites." Miss Maureen winked at her and Seth. "The two of you were definitely some of my favorites. It's good to see you, Seth. How's Joella?"

Seth cleared his throat. "She's doing fine. I'll tell her you asked after her."

Maureen turned to Bailey. "Now, I understand you could use some assistance finding accommodation for some folks."

Bailey was flummoxed by her kindness and her honesty. Nobody ever accused Maureen Laroux of being inauthentic. She always told it like it was so far as Bailey remembered. "Thank you, and yes, I do want to speak with you about rooms and possibly booking an event or two for the wrap-up."

"Lovely. Oh, and I'm assuming you've met my husband, Howard?" She nodded to the man who'd answered the door and was now busy arranging logs in the fireplace as if he planned to start a fire.

Her husband. That's right, someone had mentioned she'd recently remarried. "Yes, he introduced himself."

"I figured he had. Doesn't lose a good opportunity to meet a new friend, does Howard." She smiled. "Then it's off to the kitchen we go. I find business is best done over coffee, tea, and baked goods."

It certainly was in this town.

"I assume you and the sheriff have done some initial planning for what's to come with regard to setting up your people for filming?" Maureen motion for them to sit at the large counter on a comfortable-looking barstool covered with Naugahyde leather. The entire kitchen was double the size of most. It was set up for catering events, Bailey supposed. But it didn't come off as too industrial, though the ten-burner stainless steel stove, four cavernous ovens, along with the refrigerator that took up half the wall said differently.

Maureen didn't seem to intimate anything regarding Seth and her other than business, which was a relief. So far, everyone else she'd come across had made a comment about their past.

"We have, but I also hoped, since you are the official holiday planner, to get a day-to-day schedule of events and what time they will occur. So many of our outdoor scenes will take place around your events. I know we will intrude, so I am hoping we can either film just before the scheduled event or maybe after. We'll need local extras, so shooting while everyone is gathered makes sense. The crowd will be organic."

Maureen slid a tea tray with scones and tiny finger sandwiches toward Bailey. She'd listened quietly as Bailey spoke. "Help yourselves." It was like she'd whipped them up with a magic wand. Who had those things lying around?

"Thanks. This is lovely," Bailey said. She could feel Seth beside her, but he wasn't inserting himself into the conversation, which she appreciated. Maybe he was too busy scarfing down tiny sandwiches.

Maureen reached over and pulled out a clipboard from the built-in desk that held a large paper calendar, a corkboard that hung above it, and many, many notes with colorful pins stuck on it. This woman ran a business, lest anyone forget. "Now, let me see. I've got the schedule right here. Most of our events are consecutive daily, beginning on the tenth, besides the kickoff to Christmas, which is in just a few days. That would mean you've got just over a week until the Jingle Jog, if you're interested in filming that."

"Yes, I think we're a go for that. We might need to recruit some extras as runners, depending on how many you've got signed up. Our hero and heroine could have a scene while it's going on. I'm not sure how many changes will need to be worked in due to the change in venue," Bailey said, making notes in her notebook as she spoke.

"I can't imagine how complicated changing everything at the last minute must be," Maureen said.

Bailey attempted only to focus on what her job at hand was: securing rooms for the cast and crew, lest she become completely overwhelmed. "I try not to think about the script changes this will cause. Right now I'm doing my best to anticipate how it all will seem when everyone arrives. And make the transition as smooth as possible."

"Well, I for one, will do anything I can to assist you in your mighty objective. Because it sounds like you will require support from others." Maureen lifted her teacup as if in salute. "As far as rooms go, I can offer six. They are large and some share bathrooms. Please choose the tenants carefully, as they will be in my home. No rock stars, if you don't mind."

Six rooms. Not nearly enough. "I'll take the six rooms. Thank you. And I will be mindful of who stays here. No rock stars." But there were one or two who had somewhat high opinions of themselves. Bailey made a note to put them elsewhere.

"Is everything alright?" Maureen asked.

"O-Oh, yes." Bailey realized she'd run out of spaces for the crew.

"You made a face, so I wondered."

"Yes. Well, I don't know. I need to find a place for about twenty-five more people. One hotel is booked solid for Christmas and the other can only offer fifteen rooms." Bailey had made those calls before she'd left this morning.

"Sounds like a real pickle." Maureen frowned. Then she narrowed her eyes. "What about the camp?"

"The camp?" Bailey asked.

"Your daddy's place? The lovely camp all our kids went to in the summers? He hasn't torn it down so far as I know, has he?" Her expression was hopeful.

"N-no, he hasn't torn it down." The camp. The place where so much of her childhood was spent. The lake. Fishing with Seth. Making out with Seth. Falling in love.

A wave of beautiful nostalgia washed through Bailey.

There had been seeds of perfection during those summers. She'd taken a flashlight, a down comforter, and a kerosene heater in the winter when she'd wanted to be alone and sneaked out to her favorite cabin to read and to write.

"Bailey? Are you alright?" Seth asked from beside her.

Bailey shook her head to clear the reminiscing. "I'm fine. Just remembering all the years of camp in the summer." She stole a glance at Seth, who was staring at her. Maybe he was thinking about summers past too.

"I'll have to see what kind of shape the cabins are in. Thanks for the suggestion. I'm not sure how the crew will feel about bunks, but we might not have a choice."

Seth cleared this throat then, and said, "The cabins are in pretty good shape as far as I know. I helped Aames do some repair on some of them not long ago."

"I'll bet your studio would spring for some new sheets and mattresses if they didn't have to pay for the lodging," Maureen suggested. Then she tapped her finger to her temple as if she'd come up with a new idea. "Wait. I think Aames has rented out the cabins to groups for a few family reunions and such if I'm not mistaken, hasn't he? So, at least some of the cabins must be in decent repair."

Bailey's mind was working. *Had he mentioned doing that to her?* "Maybe. I'm not sure." New bedding, new mattresses, cleaning, heating, wood for fires. It would be a lot of work. And in the end, it would likely cost almost the same amount. But she would need to check the cabins out first.

Maureen said, "Give me your contact information and I'll send over the schedules. I will also send out a letter to the planning committee and a town email informing our residents that filming will occur at many of our usual holiday events. They will have opportunities to be part of the fun if they choose. And as you fill me in, I can let them know more about how they might become involved."

A town email? That must be quite a distribution.

Maureen walked Bailey and Seth to the enormous mahogany front door.

"That sounds wonderful. We've found it's far better to get the local residents involved and excited about the film," Bailey said. "Thanks again for your help. As soon as I know who will be occupying your rooms, I'll send you their bios."

"It's my pleasure. And, Bailey dear, while you're here, I do hope you will spend some time learning more about your beautiful mother. I know you were very young when she passed, but she was a delightful and talented lady, and you are so much like her."

Bailey could only nod. Maureen's words brought to mind her daddy's suggestion to go through her things in the attic. It wasn't fair that others knew *her* mother more than her own daughter did.

→→→≪≪≪

SETH HAD SOME paperwork for Bailey to sign, so they stopped by his office after returning from Evangeline House.

Bailey was quiet on the drive back, so he didn't try to make conversation.

"You okay?" he asked as she put the Jeep in park.

She was frowning and biting her lip, a habit he well remembered from their childhood. "Huh?" She turned to focus on him as if just realizing he was there. "Yeah. I'm fine. I've got a lot on my mind. Thinking about Camp Grandview—about the cabins."

They walked into the station through the back door since they'd parked his Jeep in its spot behind the building. "I've got the permits from the city on my desk," Seth said.

The sooner she signed them the better, so they could put down the protective tarps for the talent trailers and dozens of power cords that would run across the parking area surrounding the square. The additional electricity required to power the lights, sound equipment, and set in general was enormous. There would be on-site generators so as not to knock out the streetlights. Seth had been on top of pulling permits for everything he believed the film crew would need in addition to what Bailey had forwarded from the studio. A town like Ministry had some old laws on the books that required more local politics than most places in the country to make this all run smoothly.

He'd been able to expedite things, but there wasn't much he could do about the slow walking and talking that took place.

Time was precious and in short supply, and Bailey needed as much help from the locals as possible. If he showed his willingness to pitch in, many would follow. That's how it worked here.

Chapter Seven

THERE WAS A cute little Christmas tree in the corner, and Bing Crosby was crooning about dreaming of a white Christmas in the background as she sat down across the desk from Seth. She relaxed a little.

Is this how they broke down their suspects? Pure atmosphere.

Bailey exchanged hellos with Cheryl at the desk across the room.

He slid a folder toward her with paperwork for her to sign. "Thanks for doing all this. Looks like you've been busy on my account. I appreciate it."

"My pleasure. So, what's on your mind that's got you frowning since we left Maureen's?" he asked.

Blue eyes like none she'd ever seen to this day. *Dang it.* She was weak. "I'm short almost twenty-five rooms." Yes. Back to business.

"That's a lot of rooms. You check with the Garden Inn?" he asked.

She nodded. "Full. Christmas is pretty popular around here."

"Yeah. Cammie and her cooking show put us on the map. Then Jessica Greene showed up. What's your plan?" he asked, frowning.

"Camp Grandview might be my only option. But I don't know how well Daddy's kept it up. I *might* remember him mentioning renting it but honestly, I'm not sure."

"He did rent a couple cabins out last summer for a family reunion, I think, which is why I helped him do those repairs and clean things up. But I'm not sure how many he ended up using. Let's go out and have a look, why don't we?" he suggested.

"I didn't want to call Daddy and ask about the cabins if things were a mess. He would try too hard to make it work."

"I don't think they're in bad shape. I was surprised at how well they'd held up through the years. I mean, I know Aames has kept the structures in decent shape, but the insides weren't so bad either."

Bailey's sudden surge of relief at having a supportive partner in her rapidly changing planning roller coaster was like a shot of Valium. Her anxiety nearly disappeared for a moment because he was there. Like he'd always been. She suddenly wanted to lean into it. To him. But Bailey had been on her own for so many years now. Trusting anyone to help handle her challenges was foolish.

Even reliable Seth McKay. Reliable, and oh, so gorgeous. Still.

Bailey shook her head to snap out of it and checked the

time on her watch. "My coworker Alexis arrives at three, so I have enough time to go and check out the cabins." Hopefully he didn't get some crazy idea she was trying to spend time with him. Because she totally wasn't. It was his suggestion after all.

"You can call Aames on the way. He'll want to meet us there with the keys. Hopefully he's in the area," Seth said like a man who knew exactly how things went around here.

"If he's not nearby, I can get the cabin keys from the house," she said. "I know where he keeps them." From the day she left home, Daddy insisted Bailey keep a key to the house so she could always let herself in should she ever need to. Bailey hadn't wanted to think about what kind of scenario would require her using her house key because he wasn't around to let her in, but this wasn't the expected one, she had to admit.

"Bye, Cheryl." Bailey waved at the police chief as she exited the office. She did wonder what Cheryl must think of their exchanges with one another. Cheryl looked up from her paperwork and waved at Bailey. Her expression was pleasant and didn't show any real overt interest.

"Thanks for holding down the fort, Chief. I'll be back in a couple hours."

Cheryl smirked at Seth.

Bailey wondered what that was all about but decided it wasn't her business.

Bailey dialed her daddy's number on the way.

"Hello there, baby girl. What can I do you for?" he asked when he picked up.

"Hey, Daddy. I've got a situation with finding rooms for all the crew here in town. Maureen Laroux suggested the Grandview cabins as an option. Says you'd rented them out for a couple family reunions last summer. I think I remember you mentioning it to me."

"Yep. She's right. Can't believe you don't remember our discussion about it. I sat right on the porch and spoke with you for twenty or so minutes about it."

Bailey could believe it. "I probably had you on speaker and tried to multitask with too many tasks, if you know what I mean. Sorry about that."

He sighed into the phone. "You're forgiven. But you'd better cut me some slack when I start forgetting the things you tell me."

"Okay, deal. Now, what can you tell me about the cabins? Are they habitable? If so, how many could I get cleaned up and ready within the week for use?" she asked.

"Well, now, I'll have to go out and do a good inspection," he said. "It'll take some elbow grease, but it could probably be done."

"Seth and I are headed out there now. Are you available?" she asked.

"You don't mess around now, do you?" But he laughed as he said it so she knew he wasn't annoyed by her assumption that he wouldn't mind her barging in and taking over what she wanted and needed.

"Sorry. I'm hoping this will solve my problem. And if I see that it will, I'm going to have to dive right in and get started getting the cabins in order immediately. With your permission and blessing, that is."

"What's mine is yours. You know that. If I can make your job easier, then my day is made. Goodness knows I failed you enough when you were a little girl. I'd love to make some of it up to you now." Bailey could hear melancholy in his voice.

Uh-oh. "You were the best daddy a girl could hope for. I never worried about drowning or getting eaten by a bear," she joked, because Bailey knew by his tone, he was remembering their sad times, and didn't need to start down that path.

He chuckled. "No, you were *not* going to get eaten by a bear on my watch."

"Then we're agreed, it's all good. I'll be there in a couple minutes. Are you home?"

"I turned my truck around when you said you were coming by. Me and Groucho will meet y'all there."

"See you soon." A nice thing about Daddy's career in wildlife and fisheries, is it mostly required him driving around the county roads making sure nobody was doing anything illegal or stupid so as to endanger the animals or environment. This made his job flexible for the most part.

Back to the sentimentality. It was somewhat new for

Daddy. Bailey had noticed it during some of their recent phone calls. Anytime the subject touched on her childhood or the past, he'd made comments like he had a few minutes ago. Like, he'd not been the best father, or, Bailey had deserved better.

Granted, it hadn't always been easy being the daughter of a single dad who knew nothing about young female children. He was gruff and tough and had expected her to be as well. Bailey's feminine side was underdeveloped even though she'd had a secret love of all things pink and frilly. Pink and frilly didn't go with a tackle box and a bass boat.

Of course Daddy hadn't expected her to behave like a boy. He wasn't ignorant. He simply wasn't very aware of how to nurture her as a female. And she'd been feminine. It might have been easier if she'd been less so. Some girls were.

Joella had noticed and tried to help her with the "girly" stuff as best she could. The hair, the clothes. Joella had pulled Daddy aside a few times over the years and asked to take Bailey shopping in Huntsville. Those trips with Joella had made Bailey feel like a fairy princess. Besides the one where they bought her first bras. And stuff for her period. Those were awkward. And somewhat humiliating because Bailey worried that Seth would get wind of them.

Then she would *die*. Or so she'd thought at the time. Bailey hadn't died.

Thinking about how helpful Joella had been during some pretty important points in her developmental milestones made Bailey want to head back to the pizza joint and give her another squishy hug.

The Jeep hit the ruts without regard for her deep thoughts and jarred Bailey back to the present. Seth and Camp Grandview. She didn't want to feel like he gave her the *we're in this together* team response. They weren't. But darned if he wasn't currently bumping along right beside her. Her backup. Her safety net.

No. No. No. She'd been independent for far too long to let Seth McKay infiltrate her thoughts and emotions. Make her feel new things even. Because she would be lying if she denied that every one of her senses didn't go on high alert when he was nearby. Those eyes. Those Wranglers.

➤➤➤◄◄◄

SETH STILL LOVED Grandview. Sometimes he came here to fish, leaning against one of the many old oaks that had provided shade for all the summer campers so many years past. The five-acre lake was spring fed and filled with small-mouth bass, bream, and white perch. "Good-eatin'," as his daddy used to say.

Seth hoped she still appreciated Grandview for what it represented to the two of them. He had no expectations when it came to Bailey's temporary homecoming. She had a job to do, and so far, she was doing it full speed ahead. His wish for her this Christmas was that she could absorb some of what had been so extraordinary about her childhood home instead of treating it like a snake that would bite.

He still knew her better than anyone, well, maybe not Aames, but in a different way. They'd shared everything as kids. Hopes, dreams, and so much time together. They were soul mates, if that term even meant anything. And Grandview was as close to hallowed ground as there could be for them.

Bailey and Seth pulled their vehicles in the packed gravel area designated for parking and climbed out.

"Wow. The place hasn't changed much that I can see," Bailey said as she glanced around. "It's more weathered, and the trees are bigger." She did a quick three-sixty turn. "I had no idea Daddy kept things up so well." She was staring at the main dining hall, which was the first building in a small cluster. As kids they'd eaten meals there and done arts and crafts during the hottest part of the days.

"It's a special place for sure." Seth sometimes brought his own weed eater or mower out and spent time cleaning up the area as well. He didn't discuss it with Aames. Seth figured if Aames didn't mind his coming out and fishing here, then Seth should do some work to maintain the area. It was only neighborly. There wasn't any reason to share this with Bailey.

He heard her intake of breath when she turned and faced the water. "I've got a picture of this imprinted in my mind. It's greener, and the weather is warmer in my memories, but still the same." Their boots made a dull thudding sound as they stepped onto the dock where a single aluminum boat with a small outboard motor was tied. They instinctively walked toward the end and gazed out.

"I still come out here when the weather is nice," he said. A cold breeze blew across the lake, causing the few dry, brown leaves that were left on the trees to shake and tremble. Seth noticed Bailey's slight shiver, even though she'd worn a down jacket, but had no hat covering her silky hair.

She turned and faced him. "Why?" Her golden-brown eyes were asking as much as her words.

Did she want some kind of confession? An admission that he returned because of her? "To fish."

"Oh. Yes, of course. Do the fish still bite like they used to?" she asked, her hands deep in her jacket pockets.

"Better. Because there aren't as many folks casting lines out here as there were back in camp days."

She nodded. "That makes sense." She shivered again. "It's getting colder. Let's go inside."

"It's supposed to get below freezing tonight," Seth said. He motioned for her to precede him on the dock since there wasn't ample room for them to walk side-by-side.

Aames pulled up in his truck as they were stepping back on solid ground. The second he opened his passenger door, a giant canine burst out, but stopped short at Aames's sharp whistle.

"Wow, Dad, he's getting the hang of it. Good boy, Groucho." Bailey approached the large hound with the weird black *eyebrows.* "Should I pet him now?" she asked.

"Sure, but if he starts to jump on you, the command is a loud, 'down.'"

Bailey loved animals, dogs especially. She was a sucker for a stray of any breed. Her heart broke anytime they'd see local dogs kept in pens outside for hunting, no matter that those dogs were work dogs and well-cared for. Bailey believed they should be snuggled up next to her watching classic movies and sitcoms.

Groucho here was obviously still an excited puppy, no matter that he was taking Aames's training to heart. They threw a stick for him to chase several times to calm him before heading inside.

⋙⋘

BAILEY DID HER best to keep a straight, businesslike face during the assessment of the cabins and meeting/dining hall. Coming back here was far more impactful than she could have imagined.

Every room held memories. Some of those memories swept her away in the past and either Seth or Daddy would say her name to bring her back to the current discussion of bedding, cleaning, or repair.

The cabins even smelled the same; they were all wood, so there was the combination of pine, cedar, and spruce. The logs had come from the many acres of land Daddy owned, and he'd carefully chosen the right trees ahead of time so they could age. He'd felled them in the winter because the sap content was lowest at that time. Bailey had called him Paul Bunyan after she'd heard the story of the great ax-swinging lumberman at school in kindergarten.

He'd begun construction of the camp before her momma died and he'd nearly worked himself to death finishing it after. Camp Grandview was a product of several years of Aames Boone's blood, sweat, and tears, quite literally. So it made sense that he hadn't let it fall to ruin. And the quality with which he'd built it ensured that would take a very long time to occur.

So, as they discovered, things weren't so bad here. There was dust. And the bedding and mattresses, while covered with dust covers, still required some work. Most likely replacement. Fortunately, during the drive from the airport, Bailey noticed an outlet mall not far away. The billboard sign boasted a large factory bedding store. She always wondered why they built those malls in the middle of nowhere. Now, she was thankful it existed.

"There are six sleeping cabins with eight bunks in each one." Bailey made notes as she'd been doing since her arrival. "We'll need fresh pillows, linens, and new mattress covers." At some point, Daddy had replaced the old feather mattresses with regular ones. They were old but had been protected with covers. So, under the covers, the mattresses weren't bad. They had been slept on mostly by children and young teens.

Bailey checked her watch. Two o'clock. Alexis had texted

Bailey when she'd landed. She was an hour away by car now. Not so far from the outlet mall if memory served. "I need to call Alexis. Excuse me."

Chapter Eight

"DID YOU GET them?" Bailey asked Alexis when she
drove up.

"I wouldn't have except that outlet store still had some
'back to school' merchandise they were holding onto in the
storeroom out back. Some of them are white, some are
cream, and the rest are blue. All the pillowcases are white.
The good news is I got them for cheap."

"You're the best. Did you find the other things?" Bailey
asked.

"I got the Keurigs and the coffee pods. You can't know
the horrors of a rural Alabama Walmart, Bailey. Who should
I speak to about a raise?" It was on Alexis and Bailey to have
coffee makers and coffee and bottled water for immediate
consumption for the cast and crew when they arrived.
Everything else, food-wise, would come with them.

Bailey and Alexis would provide all the information regarding restaurants, stores, and local establishments of every
kind in the vicinity. Bailey had begun putting that list
together through her research on the internet, but before she
printed anything out, she wanted to make certain to run it

by someone local to be certain not to leave anyone out.

Basically, things had to be ready for the arrival and setup for filming. Everyone should have a place to sleep, should have references for places to eat, and maps and information about the town and its amenities. They were a moving mini-city. For this film, Epic was rolling in a catering semi-truck to be parked alongside the talent trailers, complete with a cooking and catering staff of three. Bailey wished they'd had time to source locally for catering but there simply hadn't been time to make arrangements to prepare and feed everyone three meals a day.

These were some of the things Seth was helping Bailey with. Placement of trucks and trailers and finding the additional space required to make everything work. Christmas in Ministry took up a lot of area already without a movie filming at the same time. Bailey did her best when shooting to squeeze everything in and try to minimize the ugly parts of what they did.

All their gear was black and white. The trailers and equipment. Almost everything. That way, the look wasn't messy. Tarps on the ground covered all the electrical cords for aesthetics and safety. They tried to park most buses, vehicles, and trailers behind buildings where they weren't seen by ordinary citizens walking around. And they always put up barriers to try and prevent anyone from going where they shouldn't. Security personnel were stationed strategically to help with this.

Everything at a location began with Bailey getting on the ground first and organizing spaces for everything and everyone she knew would be arriving. Sometimes both she and Alexis arrived first, and sometimes Alexis was first on location. It depended on how Mr. Stone had them working and where it was.

This was the first time they'd had a last-minute kerfuffle where the location changed in the middle of filming. Thankfully the change happened after they'd finished the interior scenes. All the exterior scenes would be shot here in Ministry. At least Bailey would be touted as the hero here and not the cause of the problems. If things went smoothly.

"Are we gonna wash all these sheets before putting them on the beds?" Alexis asked.

Bailey stared at Alexis, and then all the packages of sheets bagged in the back of the rental van. Normally the answer would have been, *of course.* But even if she did have access to several industrial-sized washers and dryers, there wasn't time or womanpower. "Not this time."

Alexis made a little sign across her heart and pulled her fingers across her lips. "Nobody's hearing it from these lips."

"That's why we make a good team. By the way, do you mind staying in the apartment with me? We're running a little tight on space here." Typically, Alexis had a room to herself for the duration of filming.

"Do you snore?" she asked.

"Not that I know of."

"Do you hog the bathroom?" she asked.

"I try not to."

"Which news channel do you watch?" she asked.

"Let's stay away from that," I replied.

"Deal."

"Great. We're staying over there." I pointed to Mrs. Wiggins's house across the street from the inn.

"Get *out*. Is it haunted?" Alexis whispered. "It's so big and so *old*."

Bailey didn't answer so as not to perjure herself—just in case. "Let's get your stuff unloaded and you can freshen up from the trip. Then we can grab something to eat—if Mrs. Wiggins doesn't sense hunger and feed us before we get out the door."

"What is this enchanted place where people feed you?"

"I'll just say, you're not in California anymore." They grabbed Alexis's rolling suitcase and smaller carry-on and made their way to the front door of the large Victorian. Bailey could've used the private side entrance, but she wanted to introduce Alexis to her landlord. Then Bailey remembered the cats—the stuffed ones—just as Alexis caught sight of the two sentinels.

"What in the holy—" Bailey shushed her as Mrs. Wiggins opened the door.

"Well, who have we here, dear?" Mrs. Wiggins asked in her kindly way.

Alexis wasn't having it. "Are there bats inside too? Oh,

heck no." She took several steps back.

"Oh, no. You didn't warn her about my babies, did you?" Mrs. Wiggins's eyebrows knit in concern and understanding. She didn't seem to take offense.

"Unfortunately, no. Give us a second, Mrs. Wiggins, will you?"

"Certainly."

"The House of Horrors in the middle of Alabama. That's where you've got me staying? I like you, Bailey. I even called you a friend. But what kind of person doesn't give a girl the heads-up about those *cats*?" Alexis was clearly bothered by the dearly departed animals.

"Calm down. I'm sorry. I should have. I forget that not everyone grew up with this sort of thing."

"This sort of thing?"

"Yes. And I'll gladly admit, the cats surprised me as well. But I grew up with a father who was a wildlife and fisheries agent. You can imagine." I put an arm around her shoulders and realized she was actually shaking.

"Y'all are a special kind of weird in this town, aren't you?" she asked.

"Tell you what. I'll put your suitcases inside and we'll go up the side entrance after we stop by the local pizza joint. You'll never have to see them again. I swear it's not as bad as it seems."

"One night. One night and if I can't sleep in that haunted mansion, I'm taking my things and sleeping in the van."

"It's a deal. But I'll make sure you don't sleep in the van. We'll find another place for you. I promise."

"You ladies need help with anything?" Seth appeared out of nowhere. Well, probably not nowhere. More likely, he sauntered over from his office across the street after watching the fiasco.

"Alexis caught sight of Mrs. Wiggins's sentinels."

He nodded. "Ah."

He turned to Alexis, who seemed to forget her upset and was staring at him. "Nice to meet you, ma'am. I'm Seth McKay, sheriff of Ministry."

He'd stuck his hand out and Alexis hadn't moved. Bailey nudged her into the present. "O-oh. Hi, I'm Alexis Dupont, coworker to Bailey here."

"A pleasure." He'd sized up the situation, apparently, and decided it required action on his part.

"How can I help?" Now, he was addressing Bailey.

"Do you mind bringing in Alexis's luggage and leaving it outside my apartment upstairs? She's a little agitated at the moment, so we're gonna head over to the Pizza Pie and grab a slice or two."

"Happy to. Maybe I'll catch up with you ladies after my shift."

"Thanks, Seth. I'll owe you one." She already owed him several, if she were honest. He'd helped her in so many little and big ways since she'd been in town, her debt was growing hugely by the day.

"It's my pleasure."

Alexis continued to stare at him, mouth slightly open. "Are you drooling?" Bailey asked.

"What? No. Of course not. Well, maybe. Aren't you? *That* man is fine, do you hear?" Alexis continued until they opened the door to the heavenly smells of handmade crust and garlic. Then she stopped and her stomach growled loudly enough for them both to hear.

"Well that changed the subject, I hope."

"Hi, girls, pick your table and I'll be right with you," Joella said with a smile.

"I've landed in weird heaven," Alexis said.

"You're right and you're starving, and now, so am I."

"Hey, honey, what can I get y'all to drink?" Joella was wearing a tie-dyed T-shirt over jeans. She had her blond hair in a messy bun. Still such an attractive woman. No wonder Daddy had a thing for her.

"I'll have water," Bailey said.

"Do you have San Benedetto?" Alexis asked.

"Sweetie, I'm not sure what that is, but I'm sure we don't have it. Sorry," Joella said.

Alexis frowned and consulted the menu. "Water from a bottle then."

"Coming right up."

Bailey understood the limitations here. "It's tap on ice or basic bottled here as far as water goes until the others arrive. You'll have to make a trip back to Huntsville to the Whole

Foods if you want anything specific. Or place an order online and have it delivered," Bailey said. This wasn't the first time they'd filmed in a small town, but it was the shortest notice they'd had. Previously, they'd been able to either bring in the specialty items or order them ahead of time.

"We're in a weird barren wasteland," Alexis said.

"I thought it was weird heaven," Bailey reminded her.

"I don't know, but that pizza better deliver on how amazing it smells."

"You're hangry, and don't worry, it will."

"So when are you going to fill me in about Sheriff Hottie?" Alexis asked, but it was more a demand.

Bailey hesitated a second. Only because she wasn't quite sure how to frame her response. "Seth is an old friend." It sounded cliché even to Bailey's ears.

"Oh. My. God. He was your freaking boyfriend. I've never seen your face like that." Alexis hooted with laughter then. "This is when being brown comes in handy. We don't blush. Well, we do but you don't notice."

Bailey leaned in and spoke in a hushed tone, "Keep your voice down. Our waiter is his mom."

"You've *got* to be kidding me. This keeps getting better and better." Joella showed up at that moment with their pizza. It was an odd time for pizza; too late for the lunch crowd and early for the dinner folks, so the place was nearly empty. Bailey guessed that's why Joella didn't have someone else waiting tables.

"This smells amazing," Alexis said, hopefully forgetting about everything else for the moment besides her hunger.

They both dug into the veggie pizza with extra banana peppers. Fortunately for Bailey, Alexis wasn't vegan, so they could share. The vegan bunch coming from California would need to stick to eating all their meals from the set's catering truck. Or they wouldn't likely find much to eat in Ministry.

"All set." While they were distracted by the pizza, somehow Seth slipped in. Both Alexis and Bailey were startled mid-chew by his sudden appearance.

Bailey wiped her mouth with one of the large white napkins. "Thanks, Seth. Want a slice?" she offered.

He eyeballed the veggies and grimaced. "Um, no thanks."

Bailey could see Alexis's gaze ping-ponging back and forth between Seth and Bailey, carefully watching for—what?

"Thanks so much for bailing me out with that situation, Sheriff. But again, who stuffs their cats, honestly? I get that country folks hunt and stuff. I even get that they like to *keep* some of their animals to look at and hang on the wall, though I'll never understand any of it, but *cats?*" Alexis shuddered again.

Seth gave a laugh. "It's not your everyday thing. We happen to have a taxidermist here in Ministry who believes that domestic pets should be given equal consideration to hunting prey when it comes to being preserved in perpetuity. At least that's his motto. It's caught on here and there."

The horror on Alexis's face was almost laughable. Almost. "How *gothic*," she said and put her hand to her heart.

"Yes. But try not to hold it against Mrs. Wiggins. She's a real sweetheart," Bailey said.

"I'll give her a chance," Alexis said, and picked up another slice of pizza. "So when are you going to tell me why we need fifty single sheets?"

"It's probably better as a show instead of tell, really. But since it'll be dark soon, I guess I'll do my best to describe the situation," Bailey said.

Alexis frowned as Bailey tried to describe her plan for housing the crew.

"Like summer camp?" Alexis asked, visibly horrified.

Seth and Bailey both nodded in unison. "Exactly like summer camp," Bailey said.

"Let's meet out there tomorrow if you're available. We can discuss some of the details regarding the permits, and I could use some recommendations for a cleaning crew and a few other things," Bailey suggested to Seth.

He nodded. "I have to be in court in the morning but I could meet y'all around noon."

Chapter Nine

S ETH GOT OUT of court just before noon. Thankfully, his testimony regarding a fireworks debacle off County Road 12 last Independence Day aligned with the other witnesses. Seth had made the arrest for the wildfire started by a group of college kids who'd drank way too much and decided shooting fireworks during a drought would be a hoot.

Ignorance didn't prevent the dozens of acres from burning or stop a local first responder's injuries. God save the youth from themselves. The judge wasn't unsympathetic to their stupidity but wanted to send a message all the same. Seth would likely have a part in the students' community service in the near future.

Right now, he wished he had that kind of young, strong labor to help to assist as Bailey's clean-up crew. But maybe they would be able to do alright by enlisting some local help. She wasn't without supporters around town, whether or not she realized it.

Last night he'd loaded up some cleaning supplies and a shop vac in the back of his SUV. And he'd sent out a well-placed email. Hopefully, they could make some progress in getting the cabins habitable to a near-Hollywood standard in time for the arrival of the crew.

As he headed out toward Aames's place, it was like old times. His family had lived right down the road growing up, and raised horses. Momma's recent move closer to town had been a solid decision. Plus, the ranch required full-time help, and now that she ran the pizza place, she couldn't keep up with it.

And there was fact that Bailey was back home, even for a little while. He couldn't put words exactly to how waking up knowing he would see her today brightened his spirit. Of course he told himself she would be out of here right after Christmas, but the idea that he would share the holidays with her made the lights on all the trees around here sparkle a little brighter.

So he was an idiot. He could admit to it. But Bailey Boone was still undeniably the love of his life. California had not ruined her to the degree he'd feared. Spending the small amount of time with her he had so far, Seth could tell she was the same old Bailey, minus the braids and freckles.

His plan was to help her achieve her goals, whatever they were, because that's how he showed love. And he could shamelessly spend time with her.

"HAVE YOU TOLD Jem?" Alexis asked as they shared a cup of

coffee in Mrs. Wiggins's kitchen and indulged on short-bread. She'd invited them to coffee this morning but had to go out soon after.

"Not yet. Not exactly," Bailey answered. Alexis was referring to the camp and the bunks they were going to house the crew in. "I will as soon as I get things a little further along."

"I can't picture it. I mean, I can, but I don't think I've got it right. I keep seeing the movie version of a kids' summer camp. And that *can't* be where you're going to put our crew."

Bailey wanted to laugh at her words. Alexis was in denial. "It's the closest thing to the stereotypical movie set for a summer camp you'll ever find," Bailey said.

Alexis stared at Bailey. "Good thing you're saving Epic's movie from ruin."

"I've kept that in mind as I've tried to work all this out." While Bailey hoped for a promotion, she wondered how it would go for her if things didn't come off smoothly. Surely the studio wouldn't hold it against her if things weren't perfect.

"And it's a good thing this place practically tastes like Christmas. It's the most Christmas-y town I've ever seen without actual snow on the ground." That was a fixable problem at least. Faux foam snow was used often and it showed perfectly in a completed film. But Bailey hadn't completely given up on the real stuff yet. Christmas miracles did happen.

Mrs. Wiggins reentered the kitchen as they cleared their plates. "Sorry about leaving you girls. I had to deliver my shortbread to the café across the street."

Alexis seemed to have forgotten all about the preserved creatures here and there throughout the house once she'd tasted Mrs. W's shortbread and fresh brew. "Thank you for feeding us this morning, Mrs. Wiggins. I can't believe how well I slept last night."

Alexis had experienced the same weirdly wonderful sleep that Bailey had starting her first night here. They'd discovered last night that part of the sofa sectional folded out into a bed. A comfortable one, apparently, because Alexis wouldn't hear of taking the bedroom, though Bailey tried her best to give it to her. Alexis convinced Bailey by insisting she stayed up late every night watching television.

They thanked their landlady again and began the day. They'd both dressed for cleanup this morning after discussing what the goals for the next few days looked like. Bailey and Alexis were to accomplish the job before Mr. Stone arrived to inspect. Alexis was to help Bailey figure out the minutiae of the objective step by step. Alexis worked in spreadsheets, numbers, and details, breaking things down in specifics.

But she wasn't above helping Bailey take down cobwebs and get rid of some dust, should that be today's objective. That was why they were such a great team.

"Remember to watch for deer and other animals that

might dash out in front of your van once we get on the dirt road. This time of the day it shouldn't be too bad, but it can get dicey at dusk," Bailey reminded Alexis. "Oh, and stay on the tracks on the road. Your vehicle doesn't have four-wheel drive." But at least the van was a heavy vehicle. It would do alright as long as Alexis took it slow.

"Will I make it out there alive?" Alexis asked, all snark.

Bailey rolled her eyes. "I sure hope so."

⟫⟫⟫⟪⟪⟪

BAILEY AND ALEXIS arrived safe and sound at Camp Grandview to find that both Seth and Daddy had beaten them there. Seth appeared to be unloading equipment and supplies from his sheriff's vehicle. Bailey nearly hit the tree watching as she pulled up.

It looked like Daddy came prepared to work as well. His small flatbed trailer was hitched to his truck. On it was a small tractor he used to mow and haul things, pressure washer, a blower, and several other power tools. He wasn't wearing his usual county-issued uniform shirt with his jeans. Had he taken a day off work to help her?

"Hi there. Thanks for coming out to lend a hand," Bailey said to them both as she neared.

"Don't mention it, baby. Who's this?"

"Daddy, this is Alexis, my coworker, and friend, of course."

They shook hands. "Great to meet you, Alexis. Welcome

to Ministry."

Alexis grinned. "I think I love this place."

"This place'll be in four-star shape in no time flat." Daddy grinned at them both. "But it's Seth you've got to thank for this."

Bailey met Seth's eyes then. "I do appreciate your going out of the way to help me. This is more than you signed up for."

He leaned toward her and answered softly enough so the others didn't hear. "I didn't sign up for anything. It's an opportunity to show you what you've missed all these years." Close enough for her to feel his breath on her cheek as he spoke the words. Each one gave her tiny goose bumps down her spine.

When he pulled away, her face was on fire. She knew this because she could feel the burning of the blood that had rushed quickly to light her up like the Christmas trees all around town.

Bailey hadn't experienced anything like this in so long it took her a minute to recognize it for what it was. And it took her another minute to recover. But his words—

She was saved from a real response by a vehicle approaching; no, two. Then suddenly, the parking area was filled with vehicles. Work trucks. "Who are all these people?" She directed the question toward both Seth and her father.

Seth appeared guilty, but—relieved? "I sent an email to a few folks in town who I thought might pitch in to help us today. Kind of a community service project to get things ready for the movie folks. I didn't know if anyone, or everyone, might show. Looks like we've got a crew of support."

Bailey didn't know whether to throw herself into his arms or tell him to mind his own business and let her handle things. She wasn't used to a man riding in on a proverbial white horse to save the day.

But right now, she would behave like the professional she was. "Thank you."

He nodded in acceptance. There was a sparkle in his blue, blue eyes. And it hit her deep. "You are most welcome."

As the volunteers gathered around them, she began to recognize faces from the past. Friends. Both women and men. There were friends from school, and parents of friends. Residents of Ministry who'd come to help. Their trucks and clothing identified them as an electrician and his assistant, a plumbing crew, window washers, pest control pros, and finally, cleaning crew. She grew warm inside. This was Ministry.

There were tears in Bailey's eyes when she realized the enormity of their hearts. "Thank you all for your willingness to juggle your busy schedules to be here, I appreciate it so much. This is what I remember about Ministry, the kindness of neighbors. Please give Alexis your invoices after we're done today." Bailey motioned toward Alexis as Alexis raised her hand and clipboard.

Dave Lane, now an electrician, who Seth and she had graduated high school with, stepped forward. "Bailey, we're not here to get paid. We're donating our time and efforts to celebrate your homecoming, and for bringing business to our little town. We understand how this will put us on the map and improve our economy. So, thanks for that. Oh, and I think he's promised pizza from the Pizza Pie later, so that's good enough for me."

There was a cheer from the group and smiles all around.

If Bailey thought she was near to tears before, this about did her in. Once again, Seth saved her.

"Alright everyone, let's work out our game plan." And apparently he had one if his own folder and notes were anything to go by.

Bailey mouthed a thank you and Seth winked at her. Like they'd behaved that way with each other forever. They had, back in the day. So, she would let it slide for now. Only because he'd saved her today. Had she really believed this would've been a manageable job for Alexis and her? They'd made lists and spreadsheets. But honestly?

The group followed Seth to the gathering hall, and they were briefed as to how this effort would go down. She listened and added a few thoughts, as did Alexis, who was very astute with details. The building had an industrial kitchen in the back where meals had been prepared for campers and staff. There were tables with benches for up to seventy-five to sit and eat comfortably.

The hall could be a good meeting spot for the cast and crew for initial briefing when everyone arrived. It was large enough but still had a warm and comfortable atmosphere. Right now, it was in need of a good cleaning and airing out. But it had real potential for use during the next couple weeks. There was a huge fireplace that could be lit as well.

The only problem Bailey could foresee was transportation getting out here for that many people.

Seth was answering a few questions members of the electrical team had while Bailey made notes about using this space as a possible film location, should any additional indoor scenes be necessary.

"Where should I start?" Alexis asked Bailey. Since Bailey had taken point on this project, Alexis was deferring to her. But Alexis was also her junior in experience, so while they held the same title, Bailey was the senior in the position.

Bailey looked up from her list-making. "Oh, sorry." She glanced around and realized that only Seth, Alexis, and she were left inside. "We have twenty-five crew to house. Use your analytical brain and go through the cabins and around the camp and help me figure out what we're missing. I know they'll be bringing a ton of supplies with them but they didn't figure on staying at summer camp. We have to make this place feel like home."

Alexis nodded. "Alright. I know what we have so far." Then she grinned at Bailey. "I have to tell you; this might be kind of fun. And if we can get things ready in time, I think it will work to our advantage, cost wise."

"I'm working on transport from here to the set. We'll need a shuttle," Bailey said.

Seth spoke up then. "I'm not sure about a shuttle, but how about a yellow hound?"

Bailey knew he referred to an old-fashioned school bus. "Will it have heat?" she asked.

"Heat, yes, but no air-conditioning."

"It's the middle of winter, so that shouldn't be a problem." Bailey envisioned riding a school bus with Seth down these dirt roads as kids. It had been a bumpy, nauseating experience. "Can we get the county to grade the road and fill some of the worst potholes at least before everyone arrives?"

"I might have some pull with the county. It's been quite some time since they've seen to the road down here." His mouth quirked up at the side, causing a reaction in Bailey's insides she didn't welcome or expect.

"And the bus, could we request one built within the decade? I remember they used to keep them forever." Bailey recalled the ancient buses running routes. And how they would break down repeatedly, and how the seats were torn and dirty.

"This all sounds problematic," Alexis said, frowning. "Can't we figure out a shuttle instead of a school bus?" she asked.

"There aren't any shuttles here in town, unfortunately,"

Seth said. "And if you rented one in Huntsville, this dirt road would likely be pretty hard on it."

"If we could get a decent bus, that would work. The road is just over a mile long."

"Let me see what I can do. Most of them are privately owned. The county has a few for prisoner transport and the like. We might be able to get one from the next county over if we're short."

"We have money in the budget to rent it, so that's not an issue," Alexis said.

"Shouldn't be a problem," Seth answered.

"I'll head over to the cabins and see what we need," Alexis said. "Catch up later."

Seth and Bailey sat quietly for a moment in the mess hall of Camp Grandview, something they hadn't done together in many years. But he was here with her again.

"Thanks for taking the lead today," she said.

"I'm glad I could help." He caught her gaze. "These people care about you, you know, Bailey. They wouldn't have come otherwise."

Bailey wasn't sure she wanted that kind of investment and connection here. "That makes me feel guilty, I think. I can pay them for their work." In fact, she might prefer it. Keeping herself from reforming bonds with people and reattaching was best. She'd managed to do it for twelve years, why start muddying things up now? She was already starting to get used to spending time with Seth every day.

"It would offend them. They want to welcome you home and show their appreciation for giving the town a boost."

"It feels a little complicated," she said, shrugging her shoulders.

"That's what I always loved about you, Bailey. You're complicated. You take nothing at face value."

She experienced a tug in her heart. She'd been so tight, so outwardly calm, but his words about their past pulled at her. "That doesn't sound like a lovable quality. It sounds difficult." Bailey shouldn't go here. She didn't want to discuss their past or how either felt about the other.

"We can't pretend there's never been anything between us," Seth said, his eyes warm.

Another tug. A loosening. "It doesn't affect anything right now. It doesn't change anything, Seth. That was so long ago. A lifetime. We were kids."

"I know. But I don't want to pretend none of it ever happened."

"Okay." She smiled at him then. "It happened."

Chapter Ten

I T TOOK THREE days. Three days of backbreaking scrub-bing, mopping, dusting, and shining to get the camp into a livable state. A workable state. There was so much wood. Wood required work. And there had been rodents. And spiderwebs.

The clawfoot tub in her apartment had been Bailey's sav-ing grace. It had been put to use every night. Between Alexis and her, they'd filled and refilled it to soak away the hours of hard labor filth. Tonight, Bailey was getting ready for Ministry's official kickoff to Christmas.

Even though she wasn't required to go, Bailey felt she owed all the people in town who'd helped them get Camp Grandview ready in the past days to celebrate the start of Christmas season with them. If she was a no-show, it might look as if she'd used them for their efforts and then ducked out. Alex, on the other hand, *had* ducked out for the even-ing.

"My nails look like I've been scratching to get out of a cave underground someplace," Alexis moaned.

"There's a nail salon in town. We can make an appointment for you tomorrow."

"I'm gonna binge on Christmas movies while you go and represent, okay?" she said.

"Don't worry, you're off the hook. This is my jam."

"You're wearing *that*?" Alexis clearly disapproved of her red turtleneck and jeans. She wore designer most of the time, aside from their cleaning binge of the last couple days.

"Keeping it simple here. I can't get too fancy or I'll be shunned," Bailey said.

"Shunned?"

"Well, yes. And I'm only slightly exaggerating. It can't seem as if I'm trying to compete for the single men in town," Bailey said matter-of-factly.

"I have the feeling everybody already knows there's only one man in town whose attention you care about, so I think you're okay to at least wear a little bling with that sweater."

Bailey felt her mouth hanging open and snapped it shut. "Is it that obvious by observing us that Seth and I have a past?" She'd gone out of her way to downplay any public emotional reactions to him.

"Um, not only a past, but an ongoing present. Y'all are smoking hot together if you're asking my opinion." Bailey wasn't sure how Alexis had come to that conclusion, but the girl was pretty astute when it came to reading situations.

"How can I make it stop?" Bailey asked, worried it might cause a problem for them both professionally. When Bailey left and went back to Hollywood, she intended to leave things as she found them. Making waves had consequences.

"Take it easy, girl. I get the feeling neither of you could make it stop no matter how you tried. Some people spark off each other. I'm guessing if you ever gave in to it, there would be real fireworks." Alexis made a motion with her hands that Bailey assumed meant to mimic an explosion.

Bailey ignored the fireworks and looked down at her watch. "I gotta go."

"Here, wear this at least." Alexis handed her a long shiny chain with an open gold star that hung just below her breasts.

"It's beautiful. Thanks." Bailey grabbed her friend in an unexpected hug. "I think this place is softening your grinchy heart. Thanks for the bling."

"Never," Alexis denied, but then she grinned. "Have fun with your people. I'll be watching through the window if I get bored."

"Feel free to join us. Ministry is nothing if not welcoming, especially during the holidays."

❖

BECAUSE BAILEY WAS so strategically living in the middle of Ministry, she had only to walk out onto the street facing the house to join the festivities. Alexis *could* see most of what was happening from their living room windows.

Before she'd had a chance to enter the fray of folks who were gathering around the humongous Christmas tree, she was nearly waylaid. "Bailey Boone, as I live and breathe, it's been a coon's age since we've seen you. I heard you were back in town."

"Oh, hi, Emma. Wow, it has been a while, hasn't it?" Bailey responded. Emma Laroux was Cammie Laroux's next oldest sister, and a former Miss Alabama, turned town pageant coach. "I understand you married Matthew Pope; he's helped us in getting things worked out in securing this location."

"Yes, that's Matthew; always helping. Glad it worked out. You're still as pretty as you were in school. Cammie said you were but she's too nice to say otherwise, so one never knows." The six-foot perfect blonde arched a brow to emphasize her point.

Bailey did her best to keep up with Emma. "Th-thanks. Tell Matthew I said hi."

"You can tell him yourself. He'll be here soon. Catch you later."

And she was gone. Had Bailey noticed a baby bump on Emma?

Bailey moved with the crowd toward the center of the town square where the annual tree-lighting ceremony would take place in a few minutes. Christmas music played on a sound system and carried throughout the area. The temps had dropped and the wind picked up earlier in the day. Bailey wore a black down vest over her red sweater but nothing on her head.

She was a little chilly. As she contemplated heading over to the table where grown elves and their smaller helpers were handing out hot chocolate, Seth appeared out of the darkness. "Hi there. I'm glad you came," he said.

How *this* man had remained unmarried in *this* town for the last twelve or so years was a true mystery, Bailey thought as she took him in, trying not to overtly stare. The jeans, the eyes, the body. Slightly more weathered than he'd been in high school. "Are you cold?" Those blue eyes now held hers.

"I was considering hot chocolate," she admitted.

He nodded toward the table and the elves. She felt his hand at the small of her back giving her a slight nudge in their direction. Bailey didn't have the strength or urge to move away. He was warm, after all.

As they sipped from the cups and slowly made their way through the crowd, several people nodded and smiled or said hello to them. Many greeted them with a "Merry Christmas!" To which she returned the greeting, as did Seth. Nobody said anything or questioned them about being together, but Bailey caught a few interested looks and overt whispers.

"Ignore that," Seth said. "They're going to talk either way."

Before she could answer, they nearly ran head-on into Joella and Daddy. "Well hi, kids. What a nice surprise. It's almost like old times," Daddy said, clearly pleased as punch. Everybody hugged and kissed. You could've seen somebody yesterday, family or not, and the greeting was the same. Hugs and kisses.

Surprisingly, she'd found L.A. to be similarly touchy-feely within the creative community, so Bailey wasn't put off by the affection sharing.

Someone called out to Daddy, and he and Joella were quickly distracted by other friends.

Seth and Bailey made their way to a spot near the massive tree, their spot, as if by muscle memory. The smell of pine filled Bailey's senses. Memories from when they were kids, coming here together for the tree lighting every year played like an old movie in her mind. Hanging ornaments and drinking way too much hot chocolate or cider. Always together.

But just as quickly, Bailey had a flashback of Seth kissing her high school best friend, Sissy, a few years back. When she'd wandered down here on a rare visit, secretly hoping to catch a glimpse of Seth. It had been stupid, sneaking around like that. But it had been a weak moment.

A tear rolled down her cheek. So unexpected that Seth wiped it away before she got the chance. "You okay?" he asked.

"Being here brings back a lot of really great memories. I hadn't expected it to hit me like this." She decided not to mention catching him with Sissy.

"I have those same memories every year when they light the tree. This year I finally get to have you here with me.

You weren't just the love of my life, Bailey, you were my best friend for my whole life. I've missed you every day."

His words gutted her, but not as much as the pain mixed with joy she recognized in his eyes. She'd known him so well. Bailey had heard Sissy was a short-lived thing.

"I'm sorry I hurt you like that, Seth. I had to go and find out where I fit in the world. It wasn't here. You remember how it was for me. I know you do," she implored him to remember. To understand. Or, at least to tell her he did. To offer some relief from her guilt for the obvious loneliness and pain she'd caused him.

"You did what you needed. There was a hole inside you none of us could fill. I guess I selfishly hoped you'd go off and figure out you couldn't live without me."

The music suddenly stopped. Someone was making announcements over the loudspeakers. Maybe Maureen Laroux. She thanked a list of people for helping plan and coordinate things this year. There was a countdown, then the lights came on. Bright, brilliant in every color. But Bailey could only focus on what Seth had said.

Instead of answering his last statement directly, she said, "I've never found anything to fill the hole. I keep trying, and some days I think I'm making progress."

He smoothed a hair that had blown across her face. "Keep trying. You just haven't found the thing that brings you peace yet."

The crowd broke into "Silent Night" then. And they

joined in. The same as they'd done all those years ago.

>>>>><<<<<

SETH FOUGHT THE urge to touch her. To hold her hand. To pull her close. *God, how he'd missed her.* Standing here in a crowd beside her was torture. He'd barely laid his hand on the small of her back earlier and his fingers had felt the slight heat from her skin through two layers of clothing. He was sixteen all over again.

For once, Bailey wasn't prickly since arriving. She was soft and vulnerable. Honest about how being back here made her feel. She'd allowed a short discussion about their past and even apologized for hurting him. This was progress for his heart that she'd pulled, still beating, from his chest twelve years ago.

Christmas had always been special for the two of them growing up. Their families shared meals during the holidays and joined in all the events happening in Ministry. They'd often been together the entire season.

"Do you remember the time they made an ice-skating rink and I broke my wrist?" Bailey asked.

He nodded and grimaced. "How could I forget? You were skating backward and showing off if I recall."

"Just because you couldn't do it doesn't mean I was showing off." Bailey tried to defend her unfortunate missteps on the ice.

"I think there might have been a spin involved, so yeah,

showing off." He rolled his eyes, and laughed.

"You sat in the emergency room for two hours with me and waited," she said, smiling.

He remembered how worried he was that she would need surgery and that it was her right hand. "I knew it would interfere with your writing. And I wanted to be the first one to sign your cast."

"My writing. Only you would have worried about that." She smiled at him in an almost sad way.

"Do you still write?" he asked. Suddenly he needed to know if she'd continued doing what she loved most.

"Rockin' Around the Christmas Tree" began to play. They'd managed to find a somewhat quiet spot to talk on a bench. "I haven't in a while. I've got a couple screenplays; stories I know would be fantastic if I could take some time and finish. I can't sit down and dedicate my attention to it the way I'd like these days."

"You used to say, 'I can write anywhere, anytime.'" His recall of her saying this was so clear. He remembered them finding her curled up in one of the cabins, her notebook open, pen swept aside, sound asleep. Aames had called Seth worried about her because she wasn't in her bed one night. Aames assumed Bailey was with Seth. The temps were below freezing that night. Fortunately, she'd thought to light the kerosene heater in the cabin.

He reminded her about the cabin incident.

A wistful smile moved across her lips. "I nearly forgot

about that. I was so dedicated to my art back then," she said. "Now, it's almost like I'm afraid it would overtake me if I fall into it. It's such a powerful thing, the allure of writing."

"It's your passion, Bailey. Maybe it's even your hole filler. Have you ever thought of that?" he suggested. The Bailey he remembered could lose herself for hours in her writing and only stop when the light disappeared. She mostly wrote outdoors, preferring natural light and a pen and paper.

"It's not a practical thing. It's something I can't do while I work toward my professional goals."

"Maybe that *is* the goal," he said. "To do the thing you love most."

"I can't. It's only a dream. And dreams don't pay the bills. Period," she said.

Chapter Eleven

B AILEY TOOK A moment to speak to Maureen Laroux and said a quick hello to Matthew Pope, her contact here in Ministry before heading back to the apartment. Seth insisted on walking her "home."

The evening had been beautiful by all accounts. The Christmas tree was magical, as it always had been, and the town was a veritable postcard, the only thing missing being a few inches of snow. And judging by the falling temps and forecast, that might change at any time. But Bailey's emotions ran high, despite the flawless kickoff to Christmas.

Seth's deliberations had gotten under her skin. He'd ripped off some festering scabs, not to be gross. But that's what he'd done. Right here in this perfect town with its perfect Christmas façade. While the carols played.

Bailey was once again vulnerable here in Ministry. He'd made her face her failure. She wasn't living her best life, though for a long time this path she'd been on was the one Bailey believed would get her where she needed to go. Eventually. Wouldn't it still? Once she had the promotion? More money? Less busywork that would allow her to write more often?

What was she truly working toward? A nicer place to live? A better schedule? She would still travel to locations after things were in place, but then would bear a heavier burden of responsibility to the studio in the next position. Right now her responsibility was to her immediate boss, who answered to the studio.

Would she still sacrifice her writing and her dreams to the next level of employment? It was something Bailey had squashed along the road to success and financial stability.

"Are you alright?" Seth asked as she unlocked the outer door to her temporary home. "You're quiet."

"What? Sure. I'm fine. Thanks for seeing me home safely, Sheriff." She tried to dismiss her deep thoughts so as not to alert him that he'd opened up this can of uncertainty and provoked her heart and mind into going places she hadn't in years.

And Seth, who was so kind to her, had admitted how much she'd hurt him and how he'd missed her through the years. That wasn't a portal to their past Bailey would allow herself to enter. Even though she'd cracked a tiny bit tonight by apologizing for her part in his pain. That unexpected tear. Allowing those special and poignant memories to creep in.

But the deep dive into her feelings for Seth? Nope. No way. It was immaterial. They had no future. No sense slogging through that.

"My pleasure, ma'am," he said in his best Southern

drawl, which did nothing for her determination to not think about him. "You get some sleep."

As she shut the door, Bailey decided the next four weeks couldn't go by quickly enough. She could return to L.A. and get back to eating better and exercising daily again. The humidity here was killing her hair, even on a cold day.

Plus, she wouldn't have Seth McKay as part of her daily routine, something she'd never have believed possible again in her lifetime. It had shoved her off her game.

As she entered the apartment, she realized that Alexis was sound asleep, with the television turned off. Bailey could hear the soft sounds of the crowd dispersing outside and barely see the tree lights filtering through their window. It was all—comforting.

She decided that after the long, physically grueling few days they'd put in, calling it a night made sense. Maybe she'd be able to put her unsettling thoughts on hold and get some sleep. Though sleep hadn't been an issue for her since coming here. It was like someone had slipped a tranquilizer in her water every night before bedtime.

Bailey had to admit, the last thing she remembered before conking out, was the piercing blue eyes of the long, tall drink of water, otherwise known as Sheriff Seth McKay.

"HEY THERE, SUGAR. So glad you found a little time to come out and visit."

"I told you I'd come out when I could," Bailey said. Groucho ran over and licked her hand like a real gentleman, so she rewarded him with lavish attention, which got entire backside and tail wagging in delight.

Today might be the only day Bailey would have to spend a little time at home with Daddy before the cast and crew arrived, so she'd left Alexis to run a few errands and grab the last-minute items they still needed to spruce up the cabins for the crew. Alexis also wanted to do some exploring around town.

"Things are coming together so I thought I'd stop by." Today was Sunday, so Daddy was usually home all day doing yard work, laundry, and basically getting ready for the week ahead. She knew this because they usually spoke on Sunday, as it was her day off as well. He'd invited her to dinner, which happened earlier on Sunday, usually midday.

"The pot roast is in the oven already, along with the potatoes and carrots. Joella and Seth will be along in about an hour. Hope that's alright." He said this as he turned toward the kitchen, not waiting for her response.

"Um, I guess. Do you need any help finishing up?" she asked.

"Nope. I've got it all under control." He smiled at her. "How do you feel about going up in the attic and looking through some things?"

Something fluttered inside her belly. It wasn't exactly fear. Worry? Anxiety? But a little thrill too. "I guess it wouldn't hurt to have a look."

"I'll go ahead and check for spiders if you want," Daddy said.

"That's okay. I'll bring a broom and knock down any webs if I see them," Bailey said. She didn't love spiders but she wasn't deathly afraid of them like a lot of people she knew.

"I haven't changed the light bulb in forever but last I checked, it worked. Everything's pretty much how it's been since you left home."

"What about Momma's things?" Bailey dared to ask.

"I haven't bothered her things either. They're all covered with sheets, same as they've been since she passed, sugar. It's all yours now."

Bailey didn't know what to say about that. Daddy never could bear to talk about Momma much. A little comment here and there. He'd grieved so hard when she died.

"Let me know what treasures you find," he said and winked at her.

"A lot of dust is what it sounds like I'm gonna find," Bailey said with a laugh, trying to camouflage her nerves as humor as she headed toward the walk-up stairs to the attic door.

As Bailey climbed them, the stairs creaked, each one with a unique timbre. She envisioned doll heads staring at her with empty eye sockets. The attic. A setting for nearly every scary movie—ever.

The door stuck a little, but probably less than it would have in summer with higher humidity. It was pitch dark and smelled a little musty. Bailey reached for a light switch, which she found on the right side. A bare bulb was installed dead center on the rafter at the house's roof peak. Daddy would have needed a pretty tall ladder to reach it. Good thing it still worked. There was enough light to illuminate the center of the somewhat large space, but the corners were hidden in darkness.

Bailey didn't know where to start. It was as if someone planned to paint in here and had covered everything to protect it from getting splattered.

She pulled back a dust cover to reveal their old sofa; blue and red plaid, the one Bailey remembered throughout her lifetime in this house. Why had Daddy kept it and not tossed it when he'd gotten a new one? Yes, he was sentimental, but this thing was well past its prime.

And yet. Part of her wanted to lie down on it and inhale the past. Despite the stains from where she and Seth had eaten pizza together on it, knowing it was "against the rules." Or the memories of her and Daddy doing a *Star Wars* binge. Bailey had spent her childhood on this sofa watching television and movies, and writing her own stories. It was a couch of memories. So, yes, she could understand why it was still here in the attic.

Bailey rolled back the dust cover into a tight ball so the actual dust would stay inside instead of dispersing into the air. That way, she could sit on the sofa while she looked through things as she found them. Next to uncover was the coffee table of the past. Same. And then the chair Daddy used to sit in. It was as if their living room had been moved into the attic. It warmed Bailey's heart, while at the same time concerning her for Daddy's state of mind in his inability to let go of the past.

The next items Bailey uncovered were a large stack of old photo albums and school yearbooks. A rush of nostalgia from her childhood threatened to overwhelm her.

"Bailey? You up here?" Seth called as he stepped through the doorway of the portal to the Boone family mausoleum.

Bailey held a photo album to her chest as he walked inside.

"Wow, it's like I stepped back into the mid-nineties. It's the Boone living room as it was," Seth said as he looked around the somewhat dim area.

Bailey smiled, but her emotions were close to the surface. The past had been preserved here in some kind of perfect way that made her afraid to breathe. "It's super weird, isn't it?" she nearly whispered.

He came around to where she sat and noticed the yearbooks and photo albums. "Are you alright?"

She nodded but her tears weren't far from the surface, so she said nothing. His presence was comforting but also added to the deep sentimental moment. He wisely didn't push her by asking more questions.

Seth grabbed a yearbook from their high school and sat down beside her on the sofa. He thumbed through and let out a low whistle. "I haven't seen these people in a long minute."

He'd given Bailey just enough time to pull herself together by distracting her from her fragile moment. "What year is that?"

"Two thousand and seven. We were juniors." He tilted the annual to show her a candid black-and-white shot of the two of them. Laughing together and holding hands.

Bailey sucked in her breath at the expression on her own face. The face of innocence and joy. Pure happiness unmarred by the intensity she'd carried around constantly, or had she? Maybe she'd misremembered some of that angst? No. She'd been angsty for sure. But perhaps she'd been happy too, possibly more so than she allowed herself to recall.

"I can't believe I was ever that young. And look at you. Such a smooth baby face. Were you even shaving yet?" Bailey laughed, then, without thinking, reached up to Seth's jaw and ran her fingers gently along the days' worth of stubble. Warm and so different than the boy she remembered. But so appealing.

Seth covered her hand with his larger one. His face moved closer to hers. She felt a hint of his breath on her lips. *Was he going to kiss her? Oh, she hoped so—*

"Hey you two, dinner's ready," Daddy called, and instantly broke whatever spell of madness was happening between the two of them, thankfully. *What was she thinking?*

Bailey pulled away like she'd been tased. "Coming, Daddy."

Seth didn't say anything about her abrupt movement away from him, but she could see in his eyes that he was disappointed. He'd wanted to kiss her. And she'd been totally on board had it happened. In fact, Bailey'd made the initial move; she'd touched him first.

He cleared his throat. "Maybe we can look around more after dinner. Looks like some treasures still to be found in here."

Bailey nodded. Somewhere up here was the real treasure; her mother's things were hidden away under the years of other items and dust covers. And now that she'd begun the hunt through the past, Bailey wasn't about to stop.

"I'm pretty determined to get through some of this stuff tonight. I don't have a lot of time before the filming begins, and I'm not sure I'll have the opportunity once that starts."

"Then we've got our work cut out for us." He pushed up his sleeves as if to show his willingness to do some heavy lifting. Then he frowned as if uncertain. "Unless you don't want any help. I get it if this is something you need to do on your own."

Did she want to tackle this attic alone? Part of her was afraid to show her fragility at what there was to uncover up here. But hadn't Seth seen that before? His muscle would come in handy for sure. "I wouldn't mind some help moving things around."

"Then it's a date. *After* we demolish your dad's pot roast."

She ignored his choice of words, and not the ones about the pot roast. "Thanks. You've been a lot of help since I've been back and I appreciate it."

He sighed loudly. "I wish you'd stop telling me how much you appreciate my help. If I see you can use a hand, of course I'll do what I can."

"Would you rather I didn't thank you and used you for labor?" Bailey laughed as she said it. They were entering the kitchen as they bantered back and forth.

"Sounds like the two of you are getting along fine," Joella said, not bothering to hide her grin.

Both Seth and Bailey stared at her with no real response.

"Okay, okay. Don't mind me. I'm sticking my foot in my mouth again." Joella breezed past with a basket of rolls.

"Now, darlin', don't you let those young'uns make you feel bad. You were only stating the obvious," Daddy said, in defense of his gal pal.

Bailey and Seth shared an eye roll at their parents' goofy communicating around them, because neither Bailey nor Seth had said a word. Their parents were acting like lovesick old people.

The pot roast was no joke though. Juicy and tender, and so flavorful; Bailey'd nearly forgotten how heavenly it was.

She'd been away from that, if nothing else, for too long. Coming home, if only for the beef, would now be a priority moving forward. Now that she and Seth had broken the ice again, and avoiding that part of her past wasn't entirely necessary, Bailey didn't have such a sense of dread at the thought of coming home.

It was as if a dam had broken and all those reasons she'd heaped up for staying away suddenly evaporated, or no longer mattered like before. The pain of the place still stung from her childhood, from her mother's disappearance (that's what death felt like), but not the being present with those who were still here. Daddy, Seth, and Joella. That was okay now.

She couldn't live here, of course, but now maybe she could visit from time to time. It was a nice realization.

"You're smiling, sugar. Anything you want to share?" Daddy asked.

"The pot roast has made me realize I should come visit more often," she said.

Daddy put a hand over his heart in dramatic fashion. "I'm hurt, I think. But if a hunk of meat will bring you home to us, I'll make one anytime you get a hankering for it. I had no idea that's all it would take," he laughed.

Bailey pushed the last carrot around her plate. "It's not just that. I'd forgotten how nice it was to sit around the table with family."

"Well, darlin', we are your family, and you'd best not

forget it," Joella said from across the table.

Seth remained quiet, but when Bailey sneaked a look, he appeared to be deep in thought.

"Anybody ready for dessert?" Daddy stood and began clearing plates now that they were all done with their main course.

Chapter Twelve

"I MIGHT NEED to nap on the plaid couch for a bit before moving anything," Seth said, covering his belly with both hands to accentuate his fullness from dinner. Of course he had no belly beyond his washboard abs.

Bailey had no plans to tell him that though. "I haven't eaten that much since the red beans and rice the night I got here. If I still lived here I'd have to figure out a way to control my portion intake and run twice as far, only uphill."

"You should see his frequent Sunday breakfasts. Oh, wait, they haven't changed since we were kids."

"There's no way I could live in Alabama; no offense." But she regretted the words as soon as she'd said them. *Why had she come out with that?*

"A lot of us manage to live here in the backwoods pretty well with internet and everything." His Southern drawl increased hugely then.

He didn't exactly sound offended, but she understood how snotty her comment must have come across. "Sorry, I didn't mean it like that. I've been in a big city for a long time. I don't have anything against my home. It's—

different." But even as she said it, Bailey knew she hadn't communicated accurately. The fact was, from the moment she'd flown off to L.A., Bailey'd moved beyond Ministry, Alabama. Or she'd tried.

"It's your life and your journey, Bailey. Only you can decide what's going to make you happy."

Why did that somehow feel like he knew something she didn't? "Are you trying to Mr. Miyagi me, oh, wise one?" she joked, making reference to one of their favorite shared movies, *The Karate Kid*. The movie had been a find from her daddy's collection, and they'd watched it over and over. Mr. Miyagi was the wise karate master in the film.

He burst out laughing. "I can't believe you even remember that."

"I don't plan what I say. It just comes out," she admitted.

"We'd better get to work or we'll be here all night," he said, still smiling at her reference. "Looks like your daddy kept everything, so maybe we'll find the old *Karate Kid* VHS tape."

Bailey looked around the attic, noticing a couple of empty sockets in the ceiling. "We need a couple more light bulbs and a ladder."

"On it." He sprinted down the attic stairs.

While he ran the errand, Bailey noticed something tallish in the corner and pulled off another dust cover. And discovered a fully-decorated artificial Christmas tree—the one from her young childhood. The one with the shiny star on top. Memories of her mother came back in sudden, shocking clarity, so unexpected in their brilliance. Momma had lifted her high to place the star on it and Daddy had secured it so that it shone bright against the colored lights. The ornaments were a mix of ones they'd made and porcelain ones that had obviously been collected from other places and people. It was an eclectic and artistic tree. A forgotten tree. It brought back emotions and memories from a child's beautiful mind. Perfect Christmas memories.

"Wow, what did you discover over there?" Seth came back, dragging a ladder in one arm and holding a couple light bulbs in the other.

Bailey pulled the smallish tree gently from its nesting spot. It wasn't heavy but she didn't want to upset the ornaments or the lights, though it was highly doubtful the lights would work after so many years. "It's our tree from before Momma died. I remember the last Christmas decorating it together. I can't believe it's still in such great shape."

There was one particular ornament that sparked her memory, a red orb with *Noel* in white on one side and a sweet snowflake on the other. It had been Bailey's favorite as a little girl. Her momma had painted it, she remembered, now, seeing flashes of the two of them in her mind, painting together. Of course, her attempts had hardly been recognizable as anything but blobs of red and green.

"Wow. What a find. Let's plug it in and see if the lights

still work." Seth gently took the tree and carried it, the ornaments making jingling sounds, across the crowded room to an outlet beside the sofa against the wall.

He plugged it in. Nothing. "I figured the lights were too old." Then, Seth tapped on a few bulbs and the whole thing lit up like magic. Bailey inhaled with wonder at the sight.

"Let's leave it on while we look through some of the other stuff," Seth suggested.

Bailey nodded, blinking back tears. The tree cast a glow around the entire attic, making the room a cozy replica of Christmas past. She couldn't stop staring at the red snowflake ornament. *Noel.*

Seth installed the two missing light bulbs overhead and doubled the brightness in the space, which allowed them to see the items along the edges of the room. The things that likely had been there the longest. Her momma's things.

As Bailey lifted a sheet that covered what appeared to be an old wooden trunk, she shivered. Something about it filled her with anticipation. As she bent down to lift the lid, the musty odor of age and dust entered her nostrils and caused her to sneeze.

"Bless you. Need some help?" Seth was at the ready to lend a hand.

The lid was heavy, but she managed to open it. "No thanks. I got it." It took Bailey a minute of rifling through to realize what she'd discovered. Several hand-bound books. Manuscripts and journals. She picked one up: MY BLUEBIRD by Valerie Boone. Something clicked in Bailey's memory. Momma had called Bailey her bluebird.

It was a child's storybook, complete with watercolor illustrations and rhyming prose. It took the reader through a series of outdoor scenarios through the eyes of a bluebird. Searching for the fattest worm in the woods, perching in the trees and building a nest, and flying high over the water. Bailey got lost in her mother's story and found herself wondering what would happen next.

But as she finished and turned the pages back to the beginning, Bailey noticed the cursive writing, *To my darling Bailey, my very own bluebird. Have a merry Christmas, angel girl. I hope you remember how very much I love you. Love, Momma*

It was dated the Christmas her mother passed away. Bailey's confusion turned to anger. *Why had she never seen this precious gift from her mother? What if she'd had it to treasure throughout her childhood?* Things might have been different had she owned something tangible. Something to hold and read. Bailey felt the love of her momma flow to her from this book. This story written only for her.

"What's wrong?" Seth realized she'd gotten quiet. He'd been on the other side of the room uncovering other items.

She could only hand him the book in response while fresh tears rolled as quickly as she could wipe them away.

Timing would have it that Daddy and Joella made their entrance at that moment.

"Well, what's going on up here?" He took a moment to

take in the furniture, the Christmas tree, and Bailey sobbing while Seth held the precious bluebird storybook. "I do believe I've stepped back in time. Sugar, what's got you so upset?"

Seth took the opportunity to hand him the book.

His expression turned sad, but he smiled. "Ah, I remember your momma working on this for you. She couldn't wait to give it to you for Christmas that year. I never knew what happened to it. She got so sick around that time and went into the hospital. I spent all my time with her because I knew I was losing her. My beautiful Valerie."

"You never thought how much this might mean to me? How I might treasure something like this from my mother?" Bailey demanded through her tears.

He shook his head, grimly. "Remember when I said I made mistakes?" he asked. "I didn't handle your momma's passing with grace, sugar. In fact, I barely remembered to feed either of us. I have a lot of regrets when it comes to you." His expression became so sorrowful.

"I remember some of it. And I know how much you loved her," Bailey said, softening a little.

"I asked friends and family to pack up everything and put it up here—" he motioned around the room—"like as it was the day she died. It's all here. Everything. I was so torn up for several years. Then, when you got older, and I wasn't grieving so much, I just never seemed to find a good time to come up here and open up the old trunks. I'd forgotten completely about the books. I would never have kept them from you."

Joella put a hand on his arm. "What a wonderful tribute to Valerie. I had no idea you'd done that, Aames. I remember how hard losing her was," she said, appearing unruffled by his deep love and grief for his departed wife.

"Thanks, darlin'," Daddy said and patted her hand. He turned toward Bailey and said in earnest, "I can only hope you love someone like that, Bailey. Just once in your life. Then you'll understand."

Bailey could only nod. What he said rang true and deep. She craved that kind of love, or at least the ability to allow herself that kind of love.

"It's okay, Daddy. I understand now why so much of my childhood is up here."

"I couldn't get rid of it until you gave me permission. I felt guilty for buying new things. You've been gone, and I felt like I needed you to say goodbye to the old ones."

Bailey laughed at that. "The plaid sofa can go for sure. I'll let you know about the rest once I go through it all."

"Deal. And I'm still sorry you never got your storybooks from your momma. She spent a lot of time writing. At night and when you were napping. Even before you were born. It was her favorite thing to do besides take care of us."

"I never knew that about her until Maureen Laroux said something about it the other day," Bailey said. "I wish I had. It makes me feel like we had something in common—a connection." Tragically so. Since Bailey left home so soon after she'd graduated high school, there wasn't a lot of time to find out much of this. People hadn't spoken to a young child about her deceased momma. At least not much.

"Oh, baby, y'all were so much alike in your creative tendencies. I hate that I never realized these were things you needed to know. It was easier to not discuss it. Easier for me, that is. It feels nice to do it now."

"Thanks, Daddy. I'm happy to hear you say that." She hugged him tight.

When they pulled apart, his eyes were misty. He cleared his throat and turned toward the colorful Christmas tree. "I'd nearly forgotten about the tree. The three of us decorated it together. We can move it downstairs if you'd like," Daddy suggested.

An idea entered Bailey's mind. "Since you've already got one, maybe I can move it to my apartment while I'm here. It's not very big."

"I can help you with that," Seth suggested.

Bailey turned to where he'd been quiet for the past few minutes while she and Daddy hashed out their issues. "Thank you."

His blue eyes twinkled. "You're welcome."

"The old folks are gonna go downstairs and sit in front of the TV while y'all finish poking around up here. All that cooking's got me needing my recliner," Daddy said.

Joella rolled her eyes and took his hand. "Come on,

Poppa Christmas."

That warmed Bailey's heart. Joella loved Daddy and would care for him no matter what. Because she had no siblings, Bailey worried for him. Now she understood he wasn't alone.

>>><<<

SETH WATCHED AS Bailey learned how deeply Aames had grieved for Valerie Boone. She'd been everything to him. Seth couldn't imagine how hard it must have been for the man to raise a needy young daughter who'd just lost her mother.

The love between Aames and Valerie was something to behold. But Seth had to admit the emotional pain he'd endured after Bailey left for college had been practically crippling. Yes, they'd been young, but that hadn't mattered to his heart. She hadn't died, but she might as well have. Yet he'd been expected to continue to breathe, get up in the morning, and behave as if almost nothing had changed.

All he could do now was help the woman he loved while she was here. Yes, he still loved Bailey Boone. He'd always understood it to be true, but sitting around the dinner table and spending time going through old things with her had crystallized it for him. It was like time hadn't passed. He couldn't decide if that made him pathetic or heroic. To love someone so much for so long without any return on his feelings.

Pathetic for sure. But he wasn't pathetic enough to tell her. Yes, he'd dated some, even given it a decent try. But he'd promised himself a long time ago that if he couldn't give a woman his whole heart, he'd be cheating them both. So, here he sat.

Once they were alone again, Bailey began looking through the box of books and items that were her mothers. "Oh, my. I had no idea she was so talented and creative," she said, wonder in her tone. "Seth, come see these."

He moved beside her to see what she was looking at. As they worked their way through Valerie's journals and writings, he understood more why learning about her mother was so important to Bailey. These were the missing pieces of her personal puzzle. They helped her to better understand herself and where she came from.

"I feel such a connection to her," Bailey said. "She says things in her journals about me as a child that I never knew about myself. That I identified letters as young as two years old. That I loved to paint and draw before I could write."

"That makes sense," Seth said. "It sounds like you were creating and trying to express yourself in symbols and color in art even before you understood what writing even was."

Bailey sat back for a minute, her eyebrows pulled down in a frown.

"What is it?" he asked.

"I've stopped. Writing. I've stopped writing. I don't even journal anymore." She stared him directly in the eye then.

Her gorgeous golden-brown gaze was steady.

"That's a darn shame. Maybe you could take some time off or go on a retreat someplace quiet and, you know, get your mojo back?" Seth wanted to only say the right thing here. Be supportive and encouraging but not too over the top. He didn't want to blow this.

"I use so many excuses. But you're right; there's no excuse. I gave up." Determination creeped into her expression. He knew that look and was relieved to see it.

He smiled. "Good. So, does this mean you've decided to get back to it?"

"I think maybe it's time. You always knew how to bring out the best in me." She leaned toward him on the sofa and he instinctively put an arm around her. They sat like that for a while. He felt her relax, her head against his chest, their hips resting against one another. It was comfortable and brought back memories of watching television together as teens. Of course, having Bailey beside him also caused other feelings within Seth. Ones he'd best ignore, knowing they'd go nowhere at the moment.

"I guess I'd better get back to the job at hand," she muttered.

"I'm not rushing you."

Chapter Thirteen

THE CHAOTIC ENTRY of the trucks into Ministry was met with the curious eyes of locals. Hollywood had arrived in Alabama amid her Christmas finery. The offloading of eighteen wheelers was done in a smelly ballet; a cloud of diesel, the sounds of hydraulic brakes, and the growl of engines. The entire downtown shook, nearly rattling the ornaments on the giant tree, reminding Bailey of a scene from Whoville as the Grinch looked on.

Some of the trucks left their entire trailers behind, while others' trailers were emptied by movers, then hauled away. The erecting of the small city that would serve the movie set had begun within Ministry. The talent trailers and honey wagon were lined up and in an organized row behind the downtown in the overflow parking lots so they weren't an eyesore to the community but were close enough to the square for use.

Several buses and a few private cars rolled in from Huntsville carrying cast members. Another couple buses transported crew. Those enormous rolling homes wouldn't make it down her daddy's dirt road with all its sharp curves, ruts, and potholes. They'd determined, while the police jury had graded the road in the past couple days, the most efficient way to move the crew all at once to and from the set would be on the yellow school bus.

The catering trucks began their magic without delay; after all, these new arrivals had to eat their next meal in Ministry. Regular diets, vegetarian, vegan. All were accommodated. A catering tent, or portable mess hall, was erected within minutes of arrival.

Before the parking and offloading of trailers and supplies, Bailey and Alexis met with the team of studio professionals—which included the executive producer, producer, assistant producer, director, assistant director, gaffer, contractor, and unit production manager—as soon as they arrived and directed them as to what and who went where.

Bailey and Alexis both had a full clipboard filled with notes and information. They also had maps of the area to show them where and how things were to be parked and put into place. It was standard procedure and they all knew their roles. That was, after they asked her and Alexis a million questions.

As soon as they'd carefully gone over everything, her boss, Mr. Stone, asked her to stay back after the others had left the bus where they'd had their meeting. "Great job, Bailey. The higher ups are impressed with how you stepped up and found this location on short notice. It's rare to have things fall through during filming. Coulda been a real mess."

Bailey understood that mess would've fallen squarely on his shoulders, whether it was fair or not. "I'm glad I had a hometown that fit the bill." She smiled at him. "So far, things have gone well. I hope the crew don't mind their accommodations." Referring to the bunk houses.

"These folks have been in rougher places in the past. Sounds like the camp setting might be only a slight inconvenience. They are mostly pretty young. We can make sure to put the most flexible ones on the top bunks." He laughed at that.

Bailey let out a breath she'd been holding. She wasn't certain of how that would be received. Hopefully once everyone got established, things would settle into a routine and an acceptable new normal.

Alexis was waiting for her with Jem who'd followed Mr. Stone out of the bus. "Everything okay?" Jem asked. "He didn't say anything to me."

"Yes. He just thanked me for bringing the filming here."

Alexis sighed loudly. "Well, that's a relief."

"Alright, time to get this party started," Jem said. Her six-foot frame in high-heeled boots had her towering above them all. She began barking orders to several crew members who worked directly under her.

Everyone went into set-up mode. After the sudden and unexpected breakdown, they'd had to do at the other location, things weren't quite as organized as they normally were. But Bailey had done her best to make this transition as smooth as possible with the help of Seth and the movers and shakers in town who knew how to get things done quickly. Thankfully, the slow walking was cut to a minimum.

➤➤➤❮❮❮

SETH HAD NEVER witnessed such organized madness. That was the only term he could come up with to describe so many large moving parts in such a small area. There were whistles, yells, and plenty of folks motioning to one another that it almost seemed like they were communicating in another language.

Bailey was at the center of it all. She wore a headset and spoke into a mic, talking and pointing, consulting her handy clipboard, unmistakably the person in charge for the moment. She'd taken detailed notes on everything he'd shown her regarding the specs she'd given him for the studio's requirements. And there had been a lot. It was all being played out in real time at the moment. Her cohort Alexis seemed to handle the details and supplies.

Impressed didn't come close to how he'd describe his reaction to watching her do her thing. She was such a pro. He'd imagined her profession as a more romantic Hollywood career. Something more creative. This—this was something gritty and loud and complicated. Akin to engineering and completing a difficult puzzle with mechanics, electricians, trucks and trailers. And so many people. He'd had no idea when she'd requested all those permits from the city that it would go like this.

He wanted to help. It's all he'd tried to do since she'd gotten into town. But Seth was at a loss here. He figured if she had any questions that needed answering, she would ask. But she'd asked so many questions up front, about generators, electrical cable, and how many feet high things erected could be according to Ministry's town ordinances, how late they could film, and some very specific items he'd had to run down with the city council.

As residents looked on in amazement alongside Seth, he remained ready to jump in at a moment's notice. "Looks like our girl's got it all under control, doesn't it?" his momma asked from beside him. She'd had to almost yell over the noise.

"Doesn't appear to need my help," Seth said, torn between pride and sulking.

"You've done your part. In fact, it's time to let her do her thing. Maybe back up a step and give her some fresh air now," Momma said.

"Are you saying I've overstepped?"

She shook her head, smiling. "I'm only saying she can take it from here. If our mayor, Ben Laroux, had been here to coordinate with Bailey, you wouldn't have spent so much time with her. This was an opportunity dropped in your lap."

"I did my job." Seth's jaw tightened in defiance at her suggestion. "Because Ben asked me to."

She put a hand on his shoulder. "I know you did. And look around. She couldn't have done all this without the hours you put in behind the scenes to get everyone on board in town. Some of those old farts wouldn't have responded to Bailey the way they did to you."

"Ben could have done it in half the time; you know that." Ben was the town's golden boy and they both knew it. No animosity; just fact.

"Maybe, but he wouldn't have worked as well with Bailey. And he wouldn't have gone so far beyond his job description to try and help her along with the additional things you've done. You did all this with love, not obligation. She knows it and appreciates it, son."

He couldn't deny his mother's words, so Seth didn't bother. "She'll never move back here. Her life is in L.A."

"You can't control what she does—only what you do. You've shown her how much you care. She's gotten a good taste of what it's like to be home. I can see the longing in her eyes to be among people who love her. We don't know what the future holds. I mean, would you ever have expected Aames and me to get together?" Momma laughed.

Seth let her words sink in. She had a few good points. No use wishing for the impossible. As he watched Bailey coordinate a complete movie base-camp setup, Seth realized how hard she must have worked to earn the trust of so many people. That was the kind of accomplishment one didn't walk away from. Yes, he hoped she'd find her writing chops again, but it would definitely need to balance with her career. She was on fire in her element out here.

Home would always be here for Bailey. Hopefully, Aames had another thirty or forty years left if his health held out. Her roots would remain. But Seth had never felt the need to move on. Especially not now that he'd been near Bailey again. *Why?* Most normal people didn't carry a lifelong torch for their first love.

"Lord-a-mercy, boy. What in tarnation y'all got us into?" Mr. Miller mumbled next to Seth.

"It's quite a sight, isn't it, Mr. Miller?" Seth refused to be baited by the crotchety old farmer with a large lump of tobacco in his cheek.

"I ain't never seen anything like this mess." A brown stream of tobacco spit hit right in front of Seth's boot. His somewhat clean boot. Seth knew Mr. Miller could direct that stream within a centimeter in any direction.

Seth cut him a look. "I just cleaned these boots. Have a little respect, why don't you?"

"I gotta believe these city slickers ain't gonna have much respect for the citizens around here. The air's already unbreathable," he complained.

"Hey, Mr. Miller, why don't you come on over and have a slice of pizza on me?" Momma suggested. "I'll even throw in a cold Dr Pepper."

"Well, I don't mind if I do, Joella." Mr. Miller smiled, his brown teeth stained from years of tobacco chewing.

She linked her arm in his and led him toward the Pizza Pie.

Momma turned back and winked at Seth, and he mouthed his thanks over getting the old grumpy goat off his back for the moment. But Mr. Miller wouldn't be the only one he'd have to deal with during the next few weeks, Seth was sure of it.

Seth turned his attention back to the scene at hand. Amid the chaos, it was hard to believe things would soon go back to normal, or semi-normal once everything got moved into place. But Bailey said all of this would hardly be noticeable beyond the area on the edge of downtown they'd designated.

Most of the equipment was moveable and the scenes would be filmed on location at the events planned in the coming days so as not to reinvent the wheel, or so the studio had said.

Bailey approached him then, her eyes bright with adrenaline. "Hi, Sheriff. The director wants to know how many runners y'all expect in the Jingle Jog?"

"I have no idea, but Maureen would know. Send him her way," he suggested. "I assume you have her contact information."

She rolled her eyes and pressed a button on her headset, the off button, he assumed. "I sent it to him, but he insisted I ask for some reason. His need to know was immediate."

"You have the pleasure of telling him I didn't know. I

assume he's a difficult one," Seth said.

She nodded. "Some are, more than others." She'd kept smiling the entire time, the dimple on the left side of her mouth making him want to lean in and kiss her. But of course he'd never undermine her like that. She was the bomb around here, commanding respect from everyone. Which made him want to kiss her even more.

"Good luck with that. Hopefully, y'all can get everything set up by dark."

She looked at her watch. "I'd better get back to work."

"Can I help?" he couldn't stop himself from asking. Because even the bomb might need some help.

"Nope, but thanks. This is all mine. But I'll let you know if I have any more questions you can't answer."

He laughed at that, watching her hips as she strode back to her position in the middle of it all.

Chapter Fourteen

B AILEY WAS CAREFUL to drive ahead of the school bus to Camp Grandview in the Jeep because of the red dust the bus kicked up. "Fingers crossed they aren't going to flip out about this," Alexis said from beside her.

"The mattresses seem to be in good shape since they've been covered. I laid down on one and was surprised at how comfortable it was after we put those thick pads on them," Bailey said. "Plus, we've got all the coffee and food stuff for them to put in the kitchen area." They'd taken a portion of the staples for the twenty-five guys who were staying out here.

"I guess we'll see. I put the 'most likely to be flexible about it' guys out here." As they'd loaded up the bus, there'd been comments about heading to prison and such.

"At least there wasn't any sign of wildlife inside the cabins. No snakeskins and such," Bailey said.

Alexis shot her a look. "You might want to keep those sort of comments to yourself when we get there."

Bailey tended to forget that not everyone had grown up like she did. With the forests and creatures great and small all around. Snakes with triangular heads and colorful stripes were the only ones to be feared or killed. Most of the others were grass and rat snakes and were beneficial. Rats were still gross but not especially a big deal unless they'd infiltrated the attic.

They pulled into the parking area at the camp and waited while the others disembarked with their bags. Seth stepped off the bus, having offered to drive.

Bailey ushered them all inside the large mess hall since the temperatures had dropped in the last couple of hours. The fire was lit, and it was toasty warm inside. The guys ranged in age from eighteen to thirty-five-ish. She knew them all, so addressing them wasn't intimidating, except that she noticed a few of them wore slightly peeved expressions.

"Hi, everyone. I realize these accommodations are slightly out of the ordinary, but since changing locations was the only way to get this film done, and Christmas is completely booked up around here, I've done the best I could last minute. This camp is situated on my family's property. I grew up going to summer camps here."

Jeff, the best boy electric snorted. "Never knew you were such a hayseed hick, Bailey."

Bailey didn't engage, but she noticed Seth step forward then check himself. She appreciated his urge to defend her, but she was more grateful that he controlled that urge in this setting, where she needed to be the one in charge and commanding respect. His behaving like an alpha male would tear that down in about a minute.

Alexis stepped forward. "You'll find everything you need. The beds are clean, with new sheets and pillows. There's a change of linens in the drawer underneath every bed. There are clean towels in those drawers as well. Let us know if you see any wildlife, either dead or still moving."

"Wait. *What? Oh, hell no*," Jeff huffed, his indignation evident. *Not such a tough guy now, eh Jeff?*

Bailey nearly choked with laughter on the swallow of water she was taking. Alexis was so good.

"On that note; this *is* my hometown. Please try to be kind to the people here. I'd like to get out without offending anyone. It's like any other small-town location we've filmed in, friendly and filled with onlookers. So be patient. Thanks. Any questions?"

"Are we going to have to sleep in bunk beds?" The best boy grip asked.

Alexis answered, "Yes. You will be in bunks. Normally you share rooms, so this won't be much different. You're mostly young so snoring shouldn't be too bad. We can find you some earplugs if the crickets get too loud."

They all stared at one another, letting that sink in, Bailey assumed. "The coffee, sodas, and snacks will be set up in here. It will be a self-serve bar so anything you normally would have is here at this location. We took enough items from craft service for y'all. Sandwiches and items available to the others will be brought here every day." These guys had already eaten right before they'd left the catering tent. Some had brought to-go containers back with them. "There's a refrigerator and a microwave in here as well."

"Okay. Let's go have a look at your accommodations," Alexis said and led a small group outside in the cold wind toward one of the bunkhouses.

Seth followed the group Bailey led without invitation. "Top bunks for the young and nimble, please." There would be three cabins in use out of the four.

Bailey was impressed with the cozy setup of the cabin when they entered. The new oval braided floor rug made the place homey along with the new bedding and gas heaters working that looked like a real fire in the grates. Daddy had long ago refitted the small chimneys with gas logs to keep the chill from the cabins at night, even in the summer.

"Hey y'all, this isn't so bad," Jeff said. "It's a pretty decent setup, Bailey. Sorry if I made fun of you earlier. I was only kidding."

Bailey nodded. "No worries."

The available bunks were claimed without any issue. "The bathrooms are through here. There are four showers and three toilets. If anyone needs the overflow bathroom, it's in the mess hall we just left."

The bathrooms were basic but functional and shouldn't be an issue. "Try not to clog the toilets, please," Bailey reminded them. "There's a plunger in every bathroom."

There were a few guys left without bunks. "The rest of

you can come with me."

When they'd finished up the tour and got everyone set-tled in, Bailey, Alexis, and Seth met back up in the mess hall. "How'd it go?" Bailey asked Alexis.

Alexis grinned. "Better than I expected. You?"

"So far, so good. As long as they don't find out we weren't kidding about the wildlife, we should be okay," Bailey joked. But she did hope nobody ran into anything more than the occasional spider or cockroach. Fortunately it was winter, and currently pretty cold, so they should be okay in that department. Most of the snakes had gone into winter hiding by now. The black bears too. No need to mention any of that.

"It all looks fantastic. I didn't hear a single complaint once they got inside the cabins. They were like little boys bunking together at summer camp," Alexis said.

"They quite literally are, minus the summer," Bailey said and turned to Seth. "You know, we couldn't have gotten this place ready without your help—"

Seth held up his calloused, long-fingered hand to stop Bailey from finishing her statement. "No more thank yous. I'm glad I could pitch in. Plus, I told Mayor Ben I'd do everything possible to make this all go smoothly."

"Well, you have, and we are in your debt," Alexis man-aged to slip in. "The change in venue was…unexpected, and our bosses nearly blew a gasket. Bailey here did some quick thinking and brought us to Ministry. So far, they are thrilled because she saved their movie and their budget."

"She's a special person," Seth said.

His intense blue gaze held Bailey's and she had a hard time breaking the connection. "Uh, it's been a long day. We'd better get back and check in for the evening to make sure they've got everything they need."

"Are we going to strand these guys out here without a vehicle in case there's a problem?" Alexis asked.

"Nah, we'll leave the bus. I know at least a couple of them have a chauffer's license and are capable of driving it. I asked the question in an email a few days ago when I knew that would be their mode of transport. This way, they won't need a driver every morning and evening. Sorry I forgot to share that detail," Bailey told Alexis. They each had communications going on as they handled their particular jobs while getting things lined up here. They cc'd each other on most emails and texts, but not all.

She flipped her hand at Bailey. "Not a thing, girl."

"Well, that solves a problem. I'm hoping you ladies will give me a ride back into town." Seth reached in his jeans pocket and pulled out a set of keys, clearly for the bus. "Where do you want me to leave these?"

"I'll run them inside," Alexis said.

She and Seth climbed in the Jeep while Alexis delivered the keys. Seth immediately posted up in the back seat. "So, two weeks until you head back to the bright lights, huh?" he asked.

Bailey nodded. "That's the plan. The filming will start the day after tomorrow and run until just before Christmas."

"Will you stay in Ministry with your daddy for Christmas once the filming's done?"

The question was legitimate, but it felt ripe with expectations. Or maybe just a little guilt thrown in for her daddy's sake. Or his? "I'm not sure. It all depends what I'm asked to do for work." So she hedged.

"Do you normally work on Christmas?"

"If we shoot a Christmas film, it's possible," Bailey replied, not sure why he thought grilling her was okay. Yes, they'd shared some moments. And Bailey couldn't deny her very strong and very real emotional entanglement when Seth was near. But he didn't get to shame her about leaving during the holidays if that's what it came to.

Maybe she was already stressing about that. And Bailey didn't need him to add to her worry that it might come to pass. While Christmas films made the studio big bank, the holiday itself wasn't exactly held as precious to her bosses as it was to those here in her hometown.

Alexis returned to the Jeep, and Bailey had to admit her relief at not having to answer any more of Seth's questions. Plus, he was way too close, sitting behind her like that. There wasn't much room, with his long legs folded up. She could smell the remnants of his aftershave, or deodorant, or whatever it was that made him smell like that. In a good way, but in a way that disturbed her peace as much as his annoying questions.

"I'm ready to see what magic the cooks have whipped up for us," Alexis said. "I'm starving." The three of them hadn't yet gotten to eat as they were discussing the plans to transport everyone while the crew was eating.

"We'd better hurry, or they'll have everything cleaned up and put away by the time we get back," Bailey said. The cooks were exceptional and exceptionally efficient. They ran a tight schedule and expected others to adhere to it.

"There's always pizza waiting for us at the Pizza Pie," Seth said. "It'll be open for another couple of hours."

"It's good to know there's that option for sure," Alexis said. "I've been craving another veggie pizza since the day I arrived."

"Momma will be glad to hear it," he said. Then, "Ow, Bailey, watch it." As she hit an unexpected rut in the road. "I thought they'd fixed that."

"I had to move over to pass a truck. Oh, that was Daddy." She honked.

"Bailey, I swear you're getting your Alabama accent back stronger every day we're here," Alexis teased. "It's pretty adorable."

"What? No, I'm not," Bailey said, horrified. She knew it to be true. She'd caught herself saying y'all many times, and several other dialectical missteps. "You'd better get me back to Cali, ASAP." She laughed but suddenly had a sinking pain in her gut. The thought of heading back to L.A. made Bailey pause.

"I don't find this conversation funny at all. In fact, it's pretty darn insulting," Seth piped up from behind her ear.

"We don't mean to o-*ffend*," Bailey said in her best Alabama accent. "It's just that I'll get made fun of if I go back to L.A. with an accent. It's happened before. Every time I spend any length of time in a Southern location, I start to drawl again."

"Well, I reckon you come by it honestly, don't you?" he drawled.

"The two of you are too cute for words right now," Alexis crooned. "I wish I'd recorded this for my social media. Can you do it again?" She held up her phone as if she wanted to capture it.

"No," Bailey nearly yelled.

"No," Seth nearly yelled at the same time.

"Oh, well, I'll be quicker next time...y'all." Then she laughed and laughed.

As they entered the outskirts of Ministry, it had grown dark and the entire town shone with Christmas beauty. "The lights are beautiful, and so colorful. I don't quite remember things being this well-decorated when we were kids. I mean it was great, but this is incredible," Bailey said.

"Every year, it's been improved upon. They add something, more lights or a new feature. It's pure Christmas town now. I think it could rival any other quaint holiday destination anywhere."

"The temperature is getting near freezing and the last time I looked, there was some possible light snow in the forecast," Bailey said. "Right on time for filming."

"Y'all better grab that while you can because it doesn't happen around here very often," Seth said.

Bailey knew this and hoped they would have at least a little snow that would stick so the special effects folks wouldn't have to break out the fake stuff. "Fingers crossed. It would sure make things easier."

Chapter Fifteen

THE WEATHER HAD called for snow. But only a half inch or so, and whether it stuck depended entirely on the temps hovering right around freezing. When Alexis whooped and hollered at five o'clock the next morning, Bailey couldn't imagine what could be happening.

"It's a winter wonderland in Christmas Town, Bailey!" She knocked on her door. "C'mon, get up!"

Bailey yawned and stretched like Mrs. Wiggins's current alive cat, Scarlett O'Hara, who she hoped was snugly inside and warm for this weather event. "Coming," she groaned.

Alexis loved snow. Bailey had discovered this fact since working with her. Bailey liked the idea of snow but working in it was not as dreamy as it appeared on camera. Good thing she'd brought her snow boots.

Then it occurred to her: The Jingle Jog was today. Rain or shine. Or snow? Bailey wasn't certain about that. Could one do a 5K in the snow?

As Bailey and Alexis drank coffee and ate cereal, they answered emails with regard to the filming schedule and locations logistics, and how things might need to be adjusted with regard to the snow. Snow was a good thing when filming a Christmas movie. But when it was somewhat unexpected, it tended to throw things into a tizzy, even before the shooting began.

Bailey and Alexis stared out the window in their pajamas together like a couple of little girls at Christmas. "Look at it. It's like a scene straight out of one of our movies. Or an old postcard." Alexis sighed at the sight of Ministry decked out for Christmas, the snow coating the roofs of the old buildings with their colorful lights and green garland with red bows. The streetlights shone with a cap of snow topping each one, the poles wrapped like candy canes with red and white on a diagonal.

"It's beautiful," Bailey agreed. It was still dark and no one stirred on the street yet, though she expected the caterers were hard at work making breakfast for the cast and crew, the producers, directors, grip and gaffer were in the electric truck working out their plans for the day. This town would all come to life earlier than Ministry was accustomed to, well before daybreak and very soon.

"We'd better appreciate its beauty for another couple minutes. Because this place is about to start hopping," Bailey said.

"Don't I know it," Alexia agreed with a sigh.

Mr. Stone normally took over once they got on location, but Bailey and Alexis had come to Ministry early, so they were the boots on the ground and knew the lay of the land here. It fell to them to get releases signed by homeowners if additional driving shots or blocking off a street from traffic needed doing.

Bailey texted Seth. *Is the Jingle Jog still on?*

Yes. Street is clear and JJ is on! I've got my running shoes and sweats ready to go…

Thanks so much.

Bailey forwarded the information to Mr. Stone.

"I guess I'll get suited up. Running in the cold isn't my favorite thing to do," Bailey said to Alexis as she placed her bowl and spoon in the dishwasher.

"I don't run, but if I did, you bet it would be today." Alexis grinned as she continued texting and emailing. "Do we know how many runners to expect with this weather?"

Bailey still didn't know. "Can you send an email or call Maureen Laroux? But wait until at least six thirty," Bailey said. "I've got to take a shower and wake up."

"Nice tree, by the way." Alexis pointed to the sweet Christmas tree Seth had helped her bring over from her daddy's attic. Bailey had removed the ornaments and they'd gently wrapped the tree, with the lights on, in plastic wrap to move it here. She'd replaced the ornaments, and miraculously the lights had come on again when it was plugged back in.

"Thanks. It was our family tree when I was a little girl. We found it in the attic." They'd been so busy since that evening, Bailey and Alexis hadn't had any time to discuss the

precious family heirloom tree with its sweet red *Noel* ornament.

"Wow, Bailey, what a fantastic find. It certainly makes
our place feel festive. I love having it here."

Bailey nodded, determined not to get choked up just
looking at it. "Me too." Bailey turned and headed toward the
bathroom, "I'll be out in twenty minutes."

Dressing for work today was slightly challenging as Bailey had agreed to run the Jingle Jog as part of the
community, and to add numbers to the event for filming
purposes, in case there weren't enough to fill things in.
Bailey ran regularly when back home in L.A., so doing this
wasn't a stretch for her. She'd only gotten in a few runs since
arriving in Ministry, due to her slothfulness. Every day she'd
intended to get up earlier to run before the day started.

Bailey dressed in thick leggings with a pair of looser running pants on top that she would likely remove just before
the race started. On top, she wore a running bra, tight tank,
long-sleeved T-shirt, and finally a long-sleeved nylon zip
jacket as a top layer. In cold weather like this, layering was
important. Unfortunately, she would need to wear her
waterproof boots with her running gear until the race began
to save her running shoes from getting soaked by the snow.

Seth said the road that the race was being run on was
clear, which meant that it should be dry by the time the race
started. The more traffic on a road during the night of a
snowfall meant there was less possibility of any slick spots

where ice might accumulate. And Bailey was pretty sure the town had taken precautions with sanding or salting the roads if snow was in the forecast ahead of the race this morning.

Ministry might be a tiny town in Alabama, but it was run pretty efficiently when it came to keeping its citizens safe. If nothing else, it had good people working hard for the right reasons. The politics weren't non-existent, but they were a micro chasm of the divisiveness in today's world. The contentious issues in Ministry hardly seemed to reflect those of the rest of the country. The biggest town hall meeting conflicts were whether or not to allow businesses to open before noon or serve wine and beer on Sundays. And there was the old fight regarding where the money for high school athletics should go. Seems the girls' basketball team was well-funded for the first time in school history this year.

Daddy kept Bailey well informed, whether or not she asked for the updates. It was heartening to learn that there was progress here, though often slower than the rest of the country.

"You ready?" Alexis asked and handed Bailey a to-go cup of coffee.

"Don't I look ready?" Bailey laughed, taking the cup. She'd put her running shoes in a tote bag that held her iPad, clipboard loaded with notes, and other work-related items she needed for the day.

"Nice hairdo."

Bailey rolled her eyes. A ponytail with a headband was

the only way to keep her hair out of her eyes when she ran. It wasn't especially glamorous, but otherwise it would drive her nuts. "Are you finished scrutinizing?"

"Yes, I'm done, and I was only kidding." Alexis nudged her in the side as they made their way out into the hallway and locked the door.

A loud yowl startled them and Alexis stifled a scream. "I'm never gonna get used to that."

Scarlett O' Hara, the calico cat stood a few feet away, staring at them with her hazel eyes.

Bailey walked over and gave her head a quick scratch. "You stay inside, Scarlett. It's cold out there."

⟫⟫⟪⟪

SETH HAD BEEN working since five a.m. making sure the streets were clear for this morning's race. The current temperature was thirty-three degrees. The snow had stopped falling but wasn't melting because the sun hadn't come out yet. It was barely six thirty but the movie people were in full swing from his perspective.

Ben Laroux, the mayor, was due to arrive at his office at the far end of the town square today. Apparently, he'd flown in last night from the trip he'd been on with his wife, Sabine. This information had come to him from Sabine's sister, Rachel, the town photographer, who was ever present at local events.

Ben's return would take some of the responsibility for

being the point person with the studio off his shoulders. But as much as Seth had kept Ben informed, Ben was walking into something he knew very little about in reality. Seth intended to be here and continue to do whatever was necessary to keep things on track with the movie folks.

"Hey there, Sheriff," Alexis, Bailey's coworker said as they entered his office. "Nice boots. I gave Bailey a hard time about hers, but yours are even better."

Bailey and Cheryl exchanged greetings, as Cheryl worked at her computer, not intending to participate in the race, which allowed Seth to take the time and not worry about missing a call.

Bailey appeared ready to run the race, apart from her snow boots. He was dressed similarly but had a pair of his old cowboy boots on. "I keep 'em for special occasions," he answered Alexis's snarky comment.

"Alexis is projecting, so don't mind her. We came to check in before heading out to the location. Thought we'd stop by the catering tent on the way. You're welcome to join us," Bailey said, her golden-brown eyes bright and so very lovely.

"I was about to head over there and see about crowd control, so I'm honored to be in such fine company." He reached down for his running shoes and a jacket.

"Cheryl, you got things covered here?" Seth asked.

Cheryl nodded and raised her hand in a wave. "Y'all break a leg."

The three of them made their way across the square to where the equipment and trailers were set up at the base camp. The three inches of snow made the town a winter wonderland. "Bailey, looking good. Sounds like we've got about a hundred runners, so plenty enough for getting some great shots. We've got releases for shooting on the main thoroughfare, and the cones and barricades are up to keep anyone from parking in those areas," Mr. Stone said.

"A hundred? Wow. I did not expect that." Bailey didn't need to run with those numbers, but since she was already dressed and ready, why not? "Okay. I'm available if you need me to bail on the race to handle anything."

Mr. Stone shook his head. "We've got Alexis here to handle anything that might come up. You go on and do the race. If you see anything along the way, you can report in on your earpiece."

He handed her a small com device to stick in her ear as a way to communicate with the team. It's how they made certain things went smoothly in real time while on set or off set filming. "Got it."

Mr. Stone turned his attention to Seth then. "I'd like to thank you for getting things ready for our arrival, Sheriff. With this unexpected snow, our first day of shooting could have been a real booger. But the streets look good and we're on schedule."

"You're welcome. Let me know if there's anything I can do."

"I understand the mayor is back in town?" the older man asked.

"Yes, sir. I expect him any time now. He's not one to allow things to happen in Ministry without making certain all goes smoothly." Seth understood he would be considered second class now that Ben was back, no matter how much work Seth had done to try and help make this a success.

Mr. Stone nodded. "I'll pass the information along to the others."

Seth assumed he meant the producers and directors and execs. Mr. Stone, he'd been told, was ultimately responsible as the liaison between the town's authorities and the studio. Though in this situation, Bailey had taken point since she had the connections in her hometown.

Now that Bailey's boss was here and Ben was back, both Bailey and Seth would fall to the background to some degree, which worked for Seth because maybe it meant he and Bailey would be able to spend a little time together without her being so stressed about her job.

Bailey led Seth over to the catering tent where she grabbed a quick breakfast burrito, a banana, and a small bottled orange juice. "Feel free to have something. You're considered part of security and included in the catering numbers."

Seth hadn't realized that. "Oh. Okay. Thanks." He'd had his usual green protein shake early this morning, but since he would be running a few miles shortly, he figured a few more calories wouldn't hurt. Not that he counted them, he just rarely ate a second breakfast. The food these chefs put out looked fantastic.

There was a breakfast buffet with eggs, bacon, English muffins, and oatmeal. Then there were omelets made to order, alongside the breakfast burritos filled with the choice of meat or not. There weren't biscuits and gravy, or grits offered, but he guessed those things were too much to ask. But they were also too heavy for a guy who was about to run a few miles.

So, Seth grabbed an apple, a protein bar, and a water for now. He could eat lunch someplace in town later in the day. The idea of running on a full belly didn't sit well.

"We can sit for a minute and eat before we head over to the staging area," Bailey said. As she unwrapped her food, she stopped and looked at him, her expression uncertain. "I'm heading over to Daddy's tonight after filming wraps up. I told him I would go through some more stuff in the attic. I wondered if you wanted to join me?" she asked.

The invitation caught Seth by surprise since it seemed he'd been the one to insert himself into her personal space every time they'd been together since she'd gotten to Ministry. "I'd be happy to join you in that '90s show."

She laughed at his pun referencing her old living room furniture dating back at least the nineties. One of the favorite shows they'd watched together was *That '70s Show*. "You're funny. Maybe you should come back to Hollywood with me."

She said it offhandedly, joking. But Seth, for a split second, got a rush of excitement at the thought of her wanting him to be with her, no matter that it was in L.A. "Better watch who you invite to follow you home. Somebody might take you up on it one day," he drawled.

"I didn't—" she sputtered.

He didn't let her finish, instead gathered their trash and headed toward the large waste bin without looking back, so she didn't see the huge grin on his face. Served her right.

⤑⸱⸱⤐

BAILEY COULD ONLY imagine the shade of crimson her face must be. He knew she was kidding. *Didn't he?* Why on earth couldn't she take better care with her words? Fortunately, he'd walked away to let her get her foot out of her mouth instead of staying around for her to insert it more firmly.

She had to admit that having him around hadn't been the *worst* thing these past couple of weeks. She'd staved off allowing herself to think about how much she would miss that. Seeing him every day, his smile, the occasional brush of his calloused hand against her back. It would have to be enough.

Inviting Seth to Daddy's house after work tonight had been indulgent and probably very stupid, but Bailey had given in to basking in the pure pleasure of his company. It was temporary and oh, so tempting to spend every minute she could with Seth before going back.

Bailey would figure out how to go back to life as it was before this opportunity had arisen. She had to admit to herself that when the light bulb in her brain had lit up with this idea for moving the film here, there was an equal amount of dread and excitement about the idea. Because Bailey had known, without a doubt, it would mean running into Seth McKay repeatedly.

"Ready?" Seth asked, cutting off her depressing train of thought.

"I'm ready to outrun you, Sheriff," Bailey replied, grinning.

"That will never happen, so shall we have a wager?" he challenged.

"I'll let you know when I come up with something good," she said. "What if you win?"

"We go on a date." His blue eyes shot sparks.

"A date?" Bailey got a tingling feeling in her belly.

He nodded, smiling. "A real one. I pick you up and we go someplace nice for dinner. Just the two of us. And I get to talk about anything I want, and you have to be honest and participate."

These were high stakes indeed, Bailey realized, and she accepted that the risk of losing meant honesty. She'd not ever allowed herself the risk of honesty. Was it a bet she was willing to make?

Bailey would simply have to outrun him, just like she'd

been doing for the last twelve years. "Fine. But if I win, you pay for dinner and I don't have to talk about anything I don't want to."

His grin showed those straight, white teeth. "Deal."

"Better make that reservation," Bailey said.

Chapter Sixteen

IT SEEMED EVERY single soul she'd missed running into since returning to Ministry had come out for the first day of filming. And that would have been super had Bailey not had to keep one eye, or ear, as it were, on her job.

They all wanted a hug, bless them. "Oh, honey. I told your daddy last week that I couldn't *wait* to see you while you were in town." Mrs. Paisley, her fifth grade English teacher, squeezed her face between large wet mittens. "Aren't you a sight?"

"It's great to see you, Mrs. Paisley. How's Ginger?" Bailey asked, trying to keep it somewhat short and sweet.

"Oh, you remember, she got pregnant her first year in community college and now I have five beautiful grands. They call me Sugar, you know?" Mrs. Paisley beamed.

"Congratulations. How wonderful," Bailey said, for lack of anything better.

"Great to see you, Mrs. Paisley," Seth said. "Bailey is needed for the race. Hope we see you at the finish line."

"Y'all run good, you hear? Tell them to point a camera this way. I want to be in the movies."

They waved and moved away, but not before Bailey was stopped another three times in similar fashion.

"You're awfully popular this morning," Seth acknowledged.

"You noticed that?" she muttered. "They all want an on-screen cameo."

Security was working to keep the non-runners from the staging area for the runners. "Or maybe they want to welcome you home, since they haven't seen you in forever."

Bailey snorted. "Unlikely."

They finally made it to where the other runners were stretching. Bailey and Seth both laced up their running shoes and placed their boots and bags in the bins for runners' belongings. Bailey immediately went into job mode, making certain everything was in place for the opening shot. The gun cracked for the competition runners. They took off and left everyone else behind at the start.

The crowd had to behave, and the rest of the runners were positioned behind the actors. The actors were getting in place now. An email was sent out to all participants ahead of time, apprising the runners of filming during the race. The competitive runners were allowed to start several minutes ahead of the others so as not to be hindered by filming.

The main hero and heroine of the film were perfect. Their hair and makeup ready for their action shot. She was blond perfection, and he was a perfect dark-skinned hero. Bailey didn't interact with the talent much as a rule. Her job rarely called for it. There would be dialogue dubbed in later after the race scene was shot. Seth and Bailey would run nearby to keep others at a safe distance, though it had been specified in the email. The director announced the scene. They all got into place, and they were off.

The actors were only being filmed running for a short time. After that, the Jingle Jog would continue as normal for everyone else. Tracking shots were done by a moving dolly, which required room to move alongside the actors, which was why people and cars had been restricted in the path needed for it to move smoothly. All of the aspects of the race would be filmed to get lots of crowd and action shots. That way the scene, complete with the actors, could be edited later to include whatever parts of the race were needed.

As the actors faded out of the race at the end of the take, Bailey and Seth continued on, pacing themselves. Neither seemed especially winded at the moment. This wasn't an especially challenging distance for Bailey normally. But it was a bit more humid here, even with the lower temps, and she'd noticed a tiny patch of ice here and there, so she was careful to watch where she stepped.

Seth didn't appear to be struggling, so Bailey lengthened her stride a little. She had driven the route and was familiar with the course, and therefore knew how much farther they had to go.

"Somebody's a regular runner, I see." Seth matched her pace beside her.

"*Somebody* has to do something to support her love of rich foods." She pushed a little harder. They were nearing the front of the herd of runners. "Looks like you've maintained your cardio as well."

"Every morning, unless it storms, and then I do it on my treadmill," he replied, having no trouble keeping up.

Bailey really didn't want him to ask her the hard questions at their shared dinner, so she turned it up another notch. They were nearing the last mile, according to the signs held up by volunteers on the periphery of the route. There were non-runners along the sidelines cheering the race participants along.

As Bailey increased her speed, Seth matched it. Until they were at a near sprint the last half mile. Well ahead of the other runners, Bailey realized they had fans rooting for them, specifically. This was no longer a friendly Jingle Jog; this was a race, plain and simple.

The cheers became louder as the finish line came into sight. Bailey realized they were the first finishers since the competitive runners' heat ended. The anticipation was high. Her breath was coming in short puffs now, but victory was in sight.

She could hear Seth's shoes pounding on the asphalt a couple feet behind her. Just. A. Little. Farther. "Bailey, can you hear me?" Mr. Stone's too-loud voice boomed in her ear, causing her to lose her stride, and her step to stutter. Bailey could feel herself flailing into the void as she quite literally tripped at a full run. Panic filled her as she worked to roll out of the fall by crouching into a ball to prevent her face from hitting the street.

For Bailey, the whole thing happened in slow motion, with Mr. Stone's agitated voice in her ear. Pain exploded in her right shoulder, cheek, knees, hands—everywhere it seemed. She heard the hush of the crowd and then Seth yelling for help.

⇉⇇

WATCHING BAILEY GO down was the most helpless moment in Seth's life. It was a bad fall. She rolled and skidded across the road. They were running at top speed, so it took a few seconds for him to turn himself around and get to her stopping place at the edge of the curb. His stomach lurched. He roared to no one in particular, "Get help!"

"Bailey! Bailey, can you hear me?" She was conscious, thank God. Her eyes were wide and her pupils were huge. She was in shock. They were both so winded from running. "Bailey, it's okay. Help is on the way. I don't want to move you in case you broke something."

"It-it hurts," she moaned. There were tears in her big brown eyes, and it nearly ripped his heart out that he couldn't take her pain into himself and away from her.

"I know, babe, I know. I'm so sorry." There were on-lookers gathered around.

"Could we get some water?"

Someone handed him a bottle of water.

He tried to give Bailey a sip of water but was afraid to move her. She coughed and sputtered. "Aagh. It hurts."

"Can you tell me what hurts?" he dared to ask.

"My shoulder. My knees," she whispered. Her teeth began to chatter and her body shook.

Seth had been first on the scene many times at car accidents and other traumas, but never for someone he loved. This was different.

"Seth, let me have a look." Seth turned to see Doctor Nick Sullivan, the head of trauma at Ministry's local hospital, as next wave of runners sped past, their collective pounding shaking the street beside them. But the paramedics who'd just arrived placed a couple orange cones beside them, causing the runners to detour around them.

"Oh, thank God you're here." Seth moved aside enough to let Nick have a look. "She says her shoulder hurts. She's pretty skinned up." Seth could hear the near panic in his own voice.

"Hey there, Bailey. I'm Nick. I saw the two of you smoke past me back there. I assume you fell at a good clip." He was gently probing her. "Seth says your shoulder might have taken the brunt of the fall. I'm going to ask you to try and relax it for me if you can."

Bailey was lying on her side drawn up in pain; her knees and elbows were badly skinned and bloody through her leggings and shirt. Both the leggings and shirt had holes in them. She had a skinned place on the side of her forehead, but thankfully it wasn't bleeding too badly. "C'mon, Bailey, let Doctor Nick have a quick look at that shoulder," Seth said gently, trying to sound soothing.

Bailey whimpered as Nick palpated both her good and bad shoulders. "I don't want to take a chance moving her around too much if she's got a fracture."

The EMTs were standing at the ready with a stretcher. They were already at the race should there be an injury. Nick and the paramedics discussed the best way of moving Bailey to cause the least amount of trauma. Seth wanted to yell at them all that she was in pain and that they should do something immediately.

He'd been pretty much pushed out of the way for the moment and wasn't dealing well with that. Just as he was about to insinuate himself next to Bailey, they lifted her onto the stretcher and then into the back of the ambulance, almost in one motion.

Seth hopped into the back the moment they got her settled. Her eyes were glazed with pain. "Hey there. You won the bet, you know. Or, you were going to before you tripped," Seth said, trying to do something to distract her.

"The cat," she whispered. "I need to move the cat out of the way."

Had she hit her head harder than they thought? "The cat? What cat, Bailey?" Maybe it was best to keep her talking.

Bailey winced in pain. "The one that's alive. Not the

dead ones. You know, Scarlet O' Hara. She's in the way."

"Mrs. Wiggins's cat?"

"Yes. Mr. Stone called me on my earpiece to tell me to get the cat out of the shot."

Seth wanted to laugh; he really did. The idea of Scarlett O' Hara sashaying through a scene being filmed, and a Hollywood producer going bonkers over it was a hoot. It made sense that Bailey would be the one called in to fix it. Locations people had to handle the local issues that interfered with filming, or so he'd been told. And Alexis wasn't a cat person; that, he'd seen for himself.

"So you tripped when Mr. Stone yelled in your ear?" Seth asked, to confirm what had brought her down. "About a cat?"

"Yes. I wanted to win, but he yelled about the cat." Her eyebrows went down in a frown.

Keeping her talking, even if it was about a cat, kept her mind off the fact that they were speeding toward the ER. Seth's hands were shaking with worry, but the fact that *she* was worried about "the alive cat," relieved his mind a little.

The ride to the hospital wasn't a long one, but the two miles seemed like twenty to Seth, who tried hard not to squeeze Bailey's skinned-up hand. Her knuckles had clearly dragged and rolled over the pavement almost as badly as her knees and elbows. She was a hot mess and he'd never loved her more. Actually, if he had to compare the two of them, Seth might be a close second to her as far as hot messes went.

Chapter Seventeen

"OOOW!" BAILEY WANTED to punch someone. "Stop that." She noticed they'd started an IV on the side of her wrist, where they pushed something for pain, or so the nurse said. Maybe the IV was on her wrist because her hand had a bandage on it. Both of them did, she was told because they were skinned from her fall.

The handsome doctor was about to go on her list. "Okay, sorry, Bailey. Let's get this shoulder X-rayed first, then we'll see what's next."

"Where's Seth?" she managed to ask through gritted teeth. The pain meds were starting to kick in, but not enough.

"Sheriff's outside. Should I call him in?" he asked, eyebrows raised.

Bailey nodded, but that hurt too. She hadn't realized how much she wanted him by her side until this moment. Needed him. "Sit tight." The doctor excused himself. "I'll send Seth in."

The door opened and Seth entered. She almost didn't recognize him. He was pale, with a deep furrow between his

SUSAN SANDS

brows. He appeared sick. "Bailey, how's the pain? Are you okay?"

Then it hit her. He was *worried*. About *her*. She'd seen him upset. And worried. But not like this. "I'm okay," she whispered, but her voice was raspy and low. She attempted to reach up to touch his face—the frown—and winced.

"What is it? Do you want me to get Nick back in here?" He hovered.

"N-no. Don't want you to worry. Stop frowning, okay?" she directed, feeling the pain meds pretty good now, though they hadn't taken the pain away, only dulled it, and her brain.

He smiled then. "You're telling me not to worry about you? Well, Bailey Boone, that's not gonna happen. I *will* always worry about you. I *have* always worried about you, so while you're lying here all banged up from a fall that's mostly my fault, I'll continue to worry about you."

"Your fault?" she slurred a little.

There was a ruckus outside. Loud male voices, or maybe just one. "Don't tell me to wait. My baby's in there. I need to lay eyes on her and make sure she's alright."

The door opened and her daddy appeared, his face resembling Seth's a few minutes ago. He moved to Bailey's bedside and removed his cap, staring down anxiously at her.

"I'm okay, Daddy," she said, hoping she sounded convincing.

"I heard you took a bad tumble, baby girl." The para-

190

medics had stabilized Bailey's shoulder by taping it to a foam board of sorts, best she could tell. What she did know was that it hurt—a lot—despite the pain meds they'd pushed as soon as the IV had gone in.

"You don't look okay to me. What are they saying?" he asked Seth.

"She might have fractured or dislocated her shoulder when she fell. They're about to take her for an X-ray," Seth answered.

The door opened, as if on cue, and a couple of very capable radiology technicians stuck their heads in and asked that Seth and Daddy clear out so they could take Bailey for her X-ray. Both were male. "We're gonna take great care of you, Ms. Winged Feet. Heard you were in an all-out foot race to smoke the sheriff and win the Jingle Jog. You know, he wins every year, don't you?" the tech named Star asked. Bailey liked him already.

Bailey laughed a little. "I'm glad that's the rumor going around." But she wasn't laughing when they bumped the breaks to her portable bed and started to move. The room spun and she thought she might get sick.

Dave handed her a barf bag and called for a dose of anti-nausea meds, or she assumed that's was it was. "Can I go with her?" Seth asked them.

"Oh, you're sweet, Sheriff, but gotta put the N and O on that. Our first-place girl here will be in capable hands. Be back in a flash," Star assured Seth. Bailey wished she could have seen his reaction to Star's uncharacteristic refusal.

"Bye, baby. Try not to throw up," Daddy said as she tried not to throw up.

>>><<<

"WHAT WILL HAPPEN if she's got a fracture, Nick?" Seth asked the doctor who'd recently settled into their community. About two years ago, Nick had been a big shot trauma surgeon at Emory University Hospital in Atlanta.

"Possibly surgery if it's necessary, but let's not get ahead of ourselves. Shoulders are tricky, depending where the injury is."

"Can you do the surgery here?" Aames asked, still a little pale.

"Yes. We're a level III trauma center now, which means we can handle most orthopedic cases. I've put a call in to Dr. Palmer, our orthopedic surgeon, for a consult. He'll have a look at the digital images and come over if the X-ray shows a fracture." Seth knew that Nick had worked hard to increase the level of care for the hospital since he'd arrived. Ministry pulled from a large geographical area of other small communities in the area, creating a pretty significant need for a well-equipped and staffed medical center.

They also had a Life Flight team on call in case anyone needed transferring quickly to one of the hospitals in either Huntsville or Birmingham. They'd had a few critical patients involved in serious car accidents whose lives had been saved that way.

Nick calmly spoke. "Bailey's going to be fine. She took a fall while running, and I realize it's scary to think she's injured and in pain, but in a few weeks, whether or not she has surgery, I predict she will be just fine."

She took a fall while running. He was right. This wasn't a life or death situation, only a scary one because it involved Bailey. "Thanks for putting things in perspective, Nick."

"Yeah, she's my only kiddo, and the thought of her suffering drives me crazy," Aames said.

"Y'all excuse me. I'll go check to make sure the images are sent to Dr. Palmer. I'll be back with you shortly."

The two X-ray techs were laughing with Bailey as they wheeled her back to her temporary room in the ER. Seth figured that was a good sign. He guessed she wasn't nauseated anymore.

But the sight of her face, with its bruised left cheekbone, which was just beginning to show, and the skinned area on her forehead with the still-dried blood on it made Seth weak in his knees. *Since when had he become so fragile?*

"Darlin', you're looking a little worse for wear," Aames said, noticing her face too, Seth figured.

The nurse, Evelyn was her name, entered the room. "Gentlemen, we're gonna clean our girl up, so why don't y'all grab a cup of coffee in our newly renovated waiting area?" she suggested; except it wasn't a suggestion, more like a direct order.

Seth needed to check in with Cheryl and make sure there hadn't been any urgent calls since he'd been gone the past couple of hours. Not a lot happened around here on a normal day besides the occasional skirmish between neighbors and fairly regular calls about unruly teens driving too fast or drinking in the woods around a bonfire. And lots of paperwork. But Seth wasn't one to eschew his duties, so he agreed to move along for the moment.

"I'll be right outside if you need me," Seth assured Bailey.

"Bye, baby. I'll be in the waiting room with Seth." Aames blew her a kiss.

By the time they reached the waiting area in the front of the hospital, a small crowd had gathered. His momma was there looking rightly worried, as much for Seth and Aames as for Bailey most likely.

Bailey's boss, Mr. Stone, and Alexis were in chairs, both busy on their phones, as they multitasked while they waited for news. Mrs. Wiggins, surprisingly sat, swinging her legs, feet not quite touching the floor. Ben and Sabine Laroux seemed to be working the room.

They all looked up at Seth and Aames's arrival, questions in their gazes. Aames smiled and waved to everyone but deferred to Seth. "Bailey's okay. Pretty banged up from her fall. She's had an X-ray on her shoulder to determine if there's a fracture. No word yet on that."

Seth felt, rather than heard a collective sigh of relief.

"So glad to hear that she'll be okay. I feel somewhat responsible. I heard the whole thing through her mic before it went dead. I must have startled her or something because as soon as I called her name, she fell," Mr. Stone said.

Seth felt a strong urge to punch the graying man in his faux-fur collared jacket and bright yellow sweater. He wore white boots and tight jeans. "Yes. She told me about the cat," Seth said. That's all he intended to say. The man could think of it what he liked.

He appeared slightly chagrined. "Yes, well, that damned cat nearly ruined our kissing scene by the Christmas tree, but we went with it."

Ben Laroux approached Seth. "Thanks for taking things on while I was away, man. I owe you big-time." He stuck out a hand and kind of pulled Seth in for a bro hug and slapped Seth on the back. "We're thinking about Bailey, man."

"Great to have you back." Seth and Ben worked closely together on an almost-daily basis. They collaborated on ideas and problem-solved when issues arose. His being away had put more responsibility on Seth's shoulders, but not anything that he couldn't handle.

His wife Sabine was a lovely person, and also the town's clinical therapist. She spoke to him, "If there's anything I can do to help, please let me know. I haven't met Bailey yet, but knowing your history, and Aames, I feel like I do."

Sabine walked over to Aames and Joella and hugged

them both. Sabine wasn't from Ministry, but she'd earned her place here. It wasn't often someone from the outside came and fit in with the locals like she had. People loved Sabine, same as they loved Ben. They were as genuine as they were popular.

"Aames, Joella, Seth, we've got Bailey's results. Y'all want to come into the conference room?" Nick indicated they should precede him down the hallway and into a small room with a few chairs. "Seth and Joella, Bailey gave permission for you to be included as a support for Aames."

That was kind of her. Normally only the closest of kin would be included.

"Bailey's got a hairline fracture on her clavicle, or her collarbone." He pointed to the spot on his jacket. "But she dislocated her shoulder, which is why she was in more pain than expected. We've reset her shoulder and put her in a sling for the collarbone. She should rest and be careful for the next couple weeks to let the tendons and muscles heal. No running races for sure. She might need help dressing, washing her hair, things like that."

"So, no surgery?" Aames asked.

Nick shook his head. "No. She should be fine if she follows doctor's orders and doesn't overdo it. I'm going to give her something for pain, some antibiotic cream, and a muscle relaxer. We've cleaned up her scrapes, but she's pretty bruised on her right hip, so be aware of that area."

"How long until she can fly and go back to work?" Seth

asked, because he had to know. He might not survive her leaving this time. But he still had to know so his heart could plan to break all over again. But not for two more weeks at least.

"After two weeks, she should be able to do what she feels capable of, but I'd give it a full two weeks before going back to normal activity," he said.

"Can she use a laptop?" Seth asked, a seed of inspiration entering his mind.

"As long as she's comfortable doing so. Sitting back with her feet up with the device on her legs might work. I don't want her at a desk hunched over. If she can type with her arm close to her body, that should be fine, otherwise, she should keep the sling on."

Aames frowned at Seth. "What are you thinking, son?" he asked.

"She's got two weeks off work, and she's stuck here in Ministry. I thought maybe she might get inspired to write."

Aames whistled softly under his breath. "You'd better be careful how you approach her with it. She's darned sensitive about her writing every time I ask her about it."

Nick cleared his throat. "I'll check on Bailey's discharge paperwork."

Seth, Joella, and Aames remained in the consult room after Nick excused himself. "She admitted the other night how much she missed writing and that she's been too busy with work to focus on it," Seth told Aames.

"Where's she gonna spend the next two weeks, do you think? If she can't bathe or dress herself, who're we gonna get to help her?" Aames asked.

Seth hadn't really thought about that. "I guess we'd better leave that up to Bailey. Momma offered, and she's got her friend, Alexis, who's her roommate."

⇶⫸⫷⇷

"I CAN WALK, you know," Bailey complained as she was wheeled toward the front entrance of the hospital. She hurt all over, despite the generous amount of pain meds they'd given her while she'd been here.

"That's what everybody says, love." The orderly was a tall, muscular black man in his fifties. Bailey sighed. No sense in arguing with him. She might need a little boost to get into the car anyway, and he looked strong enough to help.

"Sorry. I know you're only doing your job," she apologized.

They'd wrapped her in a warm blanket and told her to keep it since she wasn't able to put her same clothes back on that she'd come in with. They were torn, bloody, and dirty. Plus, her shoulder needed to be stabilized, which meant she wasn't able to raise her arms above her head currently.

The front sliding doors swished, and the cold wind hit Bailey in the face, causing her to catch her breath. Seth's SUV sat in front as her chariot of escape. He was her rescuer once again. "Hey there. I sent your daddy home."

He gently laid a large, warm jacket over her good shoulder, leaving it hanging off her injured one. "Let's get you out of here." His blue eyes held a tenderness Bailey wanted to dive deep into.

Tears filled her eyes and spilled down her cheeks. "Th-thank you for being here for me."

"Oh, hey. It's okay, babe. You're okay. Of course I was here. Where else would I be?" he asked, then went around to the driver's side of his vehicle.

The orderly helped to gently guide her toward the passenger's side. "Okay, let's take a big step up, now. I've got you on this side. Don't try to grab onto anything with this arm," he said. Seth reached from the other side and supported her hand and arm to help pull her into the car while the orderly kind of pushed from the outside. The SUV was equipped with all-terrain tires, so it was pretty high off the ground.

Bailey nearly screeched as they hefted her into the vehicle, but she realized there probably wasn't any better way. She made a point to thank the orderly for his help. His was likely a pretty thankless job much of the time. When people were sick and in pain, they forgot to be courteous.

Bailey was shaking by the time they were moving. "Are you cold?" He cranked up the heat before she said that she wasn't. "What a day, huh?" he said, sounding worried and uncomfortable.

Bailey hurt head to toe and could only think about how much she wanted a hot bath in the clawfoot tub in her room at Mrs. Wiggins's place. But she couldn't manage that alone.

She tried to relax a little to help stop the shaking. "Can you ask Joella to help me when I get home?" Bailey asked, her voice hoarse.

Seth's jaw was set with obvious worry. "Of course. She told me before she left the hospital to call her if there was anything she could do. Are you sure you want to go back to Mrs. Wiggins's place? Momma would love to have you at her house and take care of you."

Bailey shook her head. "I know Daddy wants me to come home, too, but right now I need a hot bath and a hair washing. Alexis and Joella can help me with that. All my things are there, so they can make sure I'm cleaned up and put to bed for the night." Bailey tried to give him an encouraging smile.

"Do you think the hot water will hurt?" he asked and winced as if thinking about it. She appreciated his empathy.

Bailey pulled up her hand and showed him. "They've put some kind of waterproof plastic bandages over the scrapes after they cleaned them. Said I could bathe or shower with them on and they wouldn't be a problem for a couple days. Tegaderms, I think they called them." There were large Band-Aid-looking bandages covered by clear plastic.

He nodded. "I'll call Momma and have her meet us there. Are you up for a veggie pizza? You've gotta be starving."

"Sounds amazing. Have you eaten?" she asked.

He shook his head. "I couldn't earlier. I was too keyed up. But I have to say that I'm pretty hungry now."

Chapter Eighteen

G ETTING HER OUT of the car and up the stairs wasn't pleasant, but Bailey appreciated the fact that it was a team effort. Between Seth, Joella, and Alexis, they managed to usher her banged-up self inside and into her temporary home. Mrs. Wiggins was on hand to open the doors and murmur her support and kindness.

Bailey was weak and shaky; probably from getting pain meds on an empty stomach. They hadn't given her anything to eat at the hospital in case she required surgery, which would've meant anesthesia, and that definitely worked best on an empty stomach. The nausea hadn't returned, so there was that.

The pizzas waiting on her kitchen table took top priority to anything else right now, for both Seth and her. Bailey was finally able to relax once she sat down in her own space. Still in pain, but relieved at being back here.

Groaning in pleasure, she bit into the hot, gooey slice using her left hand. Bailey almost forgot about her road rash and broken collarbone due to her pleasure of taste buds overtaking her pain signals. Seth appeared equally appreciative of his loaded meat pizza. Joella knew exactly what they both craved and had, quite literally, delivered.

"Do y'all want some of this?" Bailey asked Alexis, Mrs. W, and Joella.

They all shook their heads, hovering. Mrs. Wiggins spoke up, "Dear, I've left some shortbread and fruit for you girls in case you need a snack later tonight."

God bless the tiny sweet woman. "Thank you."

Alexis, who was standing next to her, put an arm around Mrs. Wiggins. "You're so good to us."

Mrs. Wiggins grinned and blushed. "I like having someone to take care of, what, with my family being out of town," she said. "And I wanted to apologize that my Scarlett caused a ruckus for the movie people."

Bailey wanted to laugh or to cry, she wasn't sure which. But getting angry or frustrated at the elderly woman wouldn't help. "Scarlett seems to have a mind of her own, that's for sure. Maybe she could stay up here in our apartment during filming so she can't scamper out when you open the door," Bailey suggested. Then she looked over at Alexis, remembering she didn't love cats.

Alexis nodded. "I can do that." Her expression was only slightly pained.

"Well, alright. At least I won't have to worry about her slipping past me or any of the others," Mrs. W said.

There were others who'd moved in upstairs and their sounds could be heard on the old floors. "How are your new tenants working out?" Bailey asked.

"Mr. Stone is charming. He dresses so dapper and has lovely manners. And that Jem is so *tall*. They are fine boarders. And they seem to like my shortbread."

Bailey was relieved. "I'm glad to hear it." Maureen Laroux seemed to also be enjoying the actors who'd been placed at her home. With the bed-and-breakfast amenities she provided, the talent was spoiled a little more than the rest of the crew, as they were higher on the food chain.

They finished the pizza, and Bailey could tell Seth was almost as exhausted as she was. "Hey, why don't you go on home? I've got reinforcements here." She put a hand on his arm. His oh-so-muscular arm.

He ran a hand through his hair, something he did when he was tired or stressed. "I hate to leave you."

"I know, but I need to get into the bathtub. You go. I'll text you before I go to bed." She tried to be persuasive.

"If you're sure you're okay?" His blue eyes searched hers.

Bailey nodded. "I'm okay."

He dropped a featherlight kiss on the top of her head; the only place that didn't seem to have a scrape or injury. But Bailey felt it down to her toes. It wasn't a painful sensation like all the other ones she'd had over the past several hours. His kiss was part peace and part magic.

MR. STONE HAD officially relieved Bailey of her duties

pertaining to this film. "You've done far and away more than your job description to get this one back on track. Put your feet up, and we'll call or text if we have a question we can't find the answer to."

Bailey had tried to protest. This project felt so personal, and it seemed like her future with the studio depended on its success. But that was indulgent and egotistic thinking. She was surrounded by professionals who were excellent at what they did. This film would succeed because of all of them, not one individual. Certainly not her.

Bailey had to let it go. She was injured and needed a couple weeks to heal, as much as Bailey hated the loss of control and the loss of time. The one positive, if there was one she could think of right now, was that Mr. Stone felt partly responsible for her fall and wouldn't hold it against her for not pulling her weight while she was injured. Bailey'd taken almost no time off since she'd been with Epic, so it's not as if she had a track record of slacking.

What did one do for two whole weeks without a job to do? Not that she could do much in this shape. Which brought her back to the fact that she could hardly move—because she ached all over. Joella and Alexis seemed to be hovering and waiting to see what her next move might be.

"Um, could somebody help me figure out how to take a bath?" Bailey winced as she stood up from the kitchen chair she'd been perched on since they'd arrived back at the apartment.

"You bet," Alexis said. "I'll go and run the water. Bubbles?"

"Yes, please." Bailey sighed, imagining how awesome that would be. "But how am I gonna wash my hair?" She looked at them both, hoping one would have the magic solution.

"Let's give it a lick and a promise tonight then we'll get you over to the salon tomorrow for a good scrubbing," Joella suggested. "Sound good?"

A *lick and a promise* was a term Bailey hadn't heard since she'd been a small child, and her grandmother had said it when she'd referred to doing something hastily or good enough. It brought back a warm emotion just now. All the grandparents were gone now. Momma's parents had lived far from here and she'd hardly known them. Her grandmother on her daddy's side had passed when she was twelve, but she'd been a seamstress, and they'd been close.

"I'm not sure what a lick and a promise means, but I'm assuming from context that it means we'll do our best," Alexis said.

Bailey nodded as best she could. "Yep. And that sounds perfect at the moment, Joella."

"Then we'd better get to it, sweetie," Joella said.

They all moved toward the bathroom. Alexis grabbed one of the fluffy white towels off the shelf and turned on the taps as Bailey stood helplessly while Joella began gently undressing her.

"I hope you aren't too modest, 'cause we're all about to see you naked," Joella said, trying to make light of an obviously weird situation. "Here let me help you get that sling off. Seth said to make sure you keep your arm next to your body, so no sudden moves."

"It's not every day I take my clothes off in front of someone, but if I have to, I'd rather it be the two of you right now," Bailey admitted, trying to help Joella as much as she could without moving her arm too much. She tried not to cry out in pain as they maneuvered her out of the sling.

"Aw, girl, that's some serious road rash you got going on. Yikes, Bailey," Alexis said when she saw Bailey in the buff. "Gosh, you're all scrapes and bruises, hon."

Joella's face told Bailey all she needed to know. There were tears in her eyes at seeing the shape she was in.

As she carefully stepped into the steaming hot water, aided on both sides by her people, Bailey couldn't underplay the burning sensation of the heat against her scrapes, despite the fact that the worst ones were covered with the bandages and protected from getting wet. "Owww…that really burns."

"Water too hot?" Alexis asked, reaching for the taps.

"No. It's perfect. It hurts on the road rash," she said, parroting Alexis's terminology.

Bailey eased down into the bubbles, with equal parts pain and pleasure. After a few seconds, the pain subsided. She sighed. "Thank you both for being here for me."

"Do you want some privacy?" Joella asked.

Bailey nodded. "I want to soak for a few minutes."

"We'll leave the door open and you can holler if you need us. Don't you dare try and stand up or get out without help, you hear?"

Alexis lit several candles they'd purchased and used at bath time at the end of a workday, then turned off the lights, for which Bailey was terribly grateful. "Perfect," Bailey said as the candles flickered, their light enough to see.

Bailey relaxed into the deep clawfoot tub. It was hypnotic.

One of the candles had the aroma of a Christmas tree, which brought Bailey to the fact that it was Christmastime. She was finally home for Christmas with her family. With her daddy—and Seth. And Joella. For the first time in so many years, she would have a real Christmas. She would buy presents. And they could make all the candy, and bake pies. Then, Bailey shifted in the tub, and groaned in pain. *She* couldn't do any of those things.

The idea of having an old-fashioned family Christmas had taken root though. And now that she'd envisioned how that could look, Bailey decided she wouldn't let a bum shoulder and a few scrapes and bruises get in the way of her vision. This wasn't a gift to squander.

Her feelings for Seth weren't something she wanted to ponder right now. She couldn't. Because if she allowed her mind and heart to dive deep into what she'd missed and how she'd hurt him, the self-recriminations would eat her alive.

Plus, moving forward, there still wasn't a way for a second chance. Their lives were in different places and on different tracks.

She couldn't come back here to stay. It was impossible. But she could appreciate the time they had together. Wasn't that what he'd told her he planned to do?

So instead of diving headlong into what might have been, Bailey used her relaxing bath time to make plans for a Christmas to remember.

"Are you okay? Ready to wash that beautiful hair?" Joella flipped on the light without warning.

Bailey likely splashed half the water in the tub onto the oak floors, she was so deep into her planning.

"Did I startle you? Were you asleep?" Joella asked, grabbing a second towel to soak up the water on the floor.

"Oh, sorry. I was thinking about Christmas."

"You were? I've been giving it some thought, too, while I sat there staring at your sweet tree in the living room." Joella grabbed the bottle of shampoo and conditioner from a shelf next to the tub and held them up questioningly. Bailey nodded.

"So what have you decided about Christmas?" Joella asked her as she worked.

"I want to do all the Christmas things I've missed with Daddy these past years, and with you and Seth. You know: the cookies, candy, wrapping presents, sitting by the fire on Christmas eve watching movies." Bailey closed her eyes and tipped her head back as Joella massaged the shampoo into her scalp.

"Sounds like your daddy's gonna be tickled pink. Seth too. And you know I'll do everything I can to help, being as how you're all banged up. But I'm a little worried about Seth in all this."

"Oh?" Bailey asked.

"His heart, honey. I know as sure as the sun will rise that he'll be so happy to spend a wonderful Christmas with you. He's missed you so much, you know, but your being back has cracked open his wounds. I'm not sure he'll survive going back in time like this, only for you to go back to California as soon as it's over. Have a care for his heart, won't you?"

Bailey's tears mixed with her bath water. Hurting Seth further was the last thing she wanted. "I-I thought my being here for the holidays would be good for us all."

"And it will. Just don't lead Seth down a path you can't bring him back from. That's all I'm saying. Make sure he understands you plan to go back to L.A. once you're all healed up."

For the next few minutes, using the sprayer attached to the taps, Joella worked to wash, condition, and rinse the grime from Bailey's hair. If it wasn't perfect, at least her hair smelled fresh and clean.

They didn't speak much after that. Bailey thanked Joella for helping her, and Alexis came in to help her from the tub. They dried Bailey carefully and dressed her in a pair of soft cotton button-up pajamas Joella had brought from her house. That way, Bailey didn't have to raise her arms.

They managed to get her into bed and give her her medication. Bailey called her daddy and texted Seth just as her eyelids were starting to droop.

"Yell at me if you need to go to the bathroom during the night, okay?" Alexis said.

Bailey nodded, exhausted from the day.

Joella dropped a kiss on her cheek before she left for the night. "Honey, don't take what I said as hurtful. We all want Christmas to be special with you here. I couldn't be happier. I can just see the hope in Seth's eyes and it kills me."

"I understand. But he knows I live and work in California," Bailey said, her voice becoming a little slurry from the pain meds which were also making her emotional.

"Yes, but what his brain knows and what his heart believes are in conflict, I'm afraid. I'm trying to protect him. And you." Joella smiled at her in that motherly way she had.

Bailey understood Joella's need to protect Seth after what Bailey put him through the first time. "I'll make it clear that I'll only be here until the new year. But can we make candy and cookies? Because I can't do any of it by myself."

"Of course, my dear. Just like when you were a little girl," Joella promised.

Chapter Nineteen

THE SNOW HADN'T melted because the temps were still hovering around freezing. In fact, it had snowed a little more; just enough to recreate the perfect winter wonderland without the dangerous icy driving conditions. Bailey was relieved for the sake of the filming. Snow worked well for that.

Bailey stared out as the town Christmas shopped, and bells on stores jingled every time somebody went in and out. The Ministry Inn bustled with guests, and there was an added excitement that a film shooting in town brought to the mix. It became a game to try and count how many people Bailey could recognize, and then separate them into two categories: those from Ministry, and those from the film studio. She could just barely see the movie trailers from her perch on the sofa and was having a solid case of FOMO— Fear of Missing Out.

Despite the pain in her shoulder and pretty much everywhere else, Bailey was antsy and ready to do something different.

It seemed that everyone had stuff to do besides babysit

her. They checked in routinely, brought her food, and made sure she was okay. Seth planned to come over later, but he'd gotten tied up with locals giving him a hard time about the filming getting in the way of their plans, and her daddy was dealing with some illegal night hunting that required help from Seth and his deputy.

Joella was running ragged serving her special pizza to all the extra customers who'd just gotten into town for the holidays, in addition to the movie folks, who'd now discovered her special offerings, so different from anything they'd ever tried.

So, here she sat, watching it all from the huge picture window, like an idyllic scene out of one of the very movies she worked hard to find locations for.

But something wouldn't quiet in the back of Bailey's mind. The writing. It scared her to think about opening a new file and putting words on a page. But the idea excited her as well. *Could she do it?* Maybe she could start with a pen and paper like she had as a teen.

Maybe going through her old things at Daddy's would spark her creativity. She'd written so many short stories, novels even. But they'd been left behind, just like everything else twelve years ago during her great escape. Daddy wouldn't have thrown them out, and she and Seth hadn't gotten halfway through all the things in the attic, so Bailey knew it was all up there. Waiting.

Bailey made up her mind it was time to move home to

her daddy's house after spending two days sitting still in the apartment watching the activity outside her living room window.

>>>>×<<<<

THEY SPENT A little time downtown at the kitchen shop and then stopped by the mom and pop grocery Bailey loved to shop at with Daddy when she was a kid. They didn't have everything the larger chain food stores did, but Bailey managed to find most of what she needed with Daddy standing by to pull it down and load the cart for her.

How she'd hated having to rely on him to do nearly everything for her. But he seemed so happy to spend the time with her that she finally relaxed and enjoyed the cheerful Christmas music playing in the background at the store and embraced the well wishes from old friends and acquaintances who were there.

She had to let her guard down. Because that's what her issue was; keeping everyone at arm's length. Defenses were built to last, in her case, and they were mistaken for snobbery. And Bailey had to admit, living in L.A., there was a large degree of snobbery toward the American South that she'd managed to deflect with as much good grace as possible over the years.

But her people were here. She was from here. And while her accent was still remarked upon and snickered at regularly in California, Bailey had been torn between an enlightened attitude and her roots. Getting out of a small town of any kind produced a fair amount of exposure to different cultures, people, foods, and ideas, and thus, enlightenment.

But coming back this time, she'd noticed change here. More products for those with food allergies on the store shelves; more faces of color around town. A tattoo parlor? Folks with blue streaks in their hair. Her long-deceased grandmother would have called them hippies.

So Bailey tried to relax and accept her hometown people. Desiring to believe they didn't just crave an appearance in the movie being shot because she had *connections*. Maybe they *were* happy to see her after twelve years.

She and Daddy had some nice interactions with folks while they shopped. Until Bailey's pain meds wore off. Then, she suggested they head home through the maze of Christmas cheer.

Seth had caught them just as they were climbing into Daddy's truck. "Hey there. Can I give you a hand?" he'd asked.

Bailey was so grateful for his appearance she'd nearly wept. She wasn't sure how to get up that high with only one arm. Bailey had managed it earlier, but she was tiring now, plus, he smelled so nice. "Thanks. I got down okay, but I wondered how I was going to get back inside."

"Looks like y'all bought the store out," he remarked as he pretty much picked her up and lifted her inside the truck. He might have cuddled her just a bit on the way up, but she wasn't going to call him out on that. Because she *might* have leaned into him during said cuddle.

"Thanks for the rescue," she said. "And yes, we did buy a few things. I figured if I was going to be around for Christmas, we might as well spend some time baking and candy making.

"*Mmmm.* Sounds delicious."

Seth had an undeniable sweet tooth. He seriously loved fudge, if she remembered correctly. "We might share," she said and grinned at him, but it might have been more like a grimace since her hip and shoulder were screaming at her.

"You okay?" He appeared concerned.

"I'm headed home for my pain pill," she said tightly.

"We've got your pills here, honey. And look, you've got some water," Daddy said. He handed her both items that were in the back of the cab of the truck.

The pain had hit so suddenly she wasn't thinking clearly. "Thanks, Daddy. I'm glad you've got me covered."

"Y'all go on home then. I'll see you later." He kissed her on her head like he'd done after she'd fallen at the race.

"Thanks again for the boost."

Chapter Twenty

"DARLIN', YOU OKAY?" Daddy asked for about the tenth time, after hitting every rut in his dirt road. They'd graded it, but it still needed some serious work.

Bailey gritted her teeth and tried not to groan in pain at every bump and jarring vibration. "Fine, Daddy."

"Do you want to run by the camp and say hello to the guys? They've been asking after you." It was almost dark, and about time for them to have gotten back to their lodging at Grandview.

Daddy had taken her to run a couple errands before they'd hit the gravel road, and Bailey didn't think she could endure even another five minutes in the truck. "Maybe we can go tomorrow. I think I need to get off this road."

"Gosh, I'm sorry. I know it's a pain."

"It's not your fault. At least it's better than it was before." Thank heaven for small blessings.

"Well, let's get you inside then." Daddy came around to her side of the car to help her out. She was hard to help because anywhere anyone touched her there was either a bruise or a scrape, so Bailey slid slowly down from the seat to the ground with Daddy kind of spotting her.

Once she got her footing, she held his hand using her uninjured left side. He'd improved the driveway in recent years by adding some pea gravel and landscape timbers. During Bailey's lifetime here it had been the same as the road. Red dirt and rocks. There were very few paved surfaces outside the city limits of Ministry.

It was a rural community, and it had stayed that way. Sure they now had the internet and cable television, which had brought in some new information and new ideas to the decidedly small-minded small town. But they were still in rural Alabama.

"Where's Groucho?" Bailey asked, wondering why they'd not been greeted by the enthusiastic welcoming canine.

"I made him stay in the house. In fact, I'd better go on in first and make sure he's secured in case he gets excited to see you. Sit right here on the swing while I take care of him."

They'd maneuvered her up the front porch steps easily enough, but one tap from a dog's excited paw with some weight behind it might send her right back down them. "Got it." So, Bailey sat on the front porch and gently swung to and fro, her jacket hanging off her bum shoulder.

It was so quiet out here it seemed unnatural. Not a single sound besides the rustling of nature, which could be anything. Daddy's front yard might yield a deer or a family of squirrels at any moment. So unlike what she'd become used to in the city. A bright red cardinal hopped along the ground, its jerky movements capturing Bailey's attention.

She sighed. Her thoughts and emotions were a jumble right now. Bailey wished she could write them down. That's what she did when she was younger; it was how she processed her emotions. A notebook and a pen.

"Okay, I've got that giant squared away with a bone. He'll be a happy dude for at least a half hour," Daddy said as he came bursting out the front door.

"Hey, Daddy," Bailey started.

"Yeah, darlin'?" He sat next to her on the swing.

"Do you think I could get up to the attic?" she asked.

He frowned. "Now why do you need to go there? I thought you'd found what you were looking for."

"I barely got started. I hadn't even found all my journals and things."

He nodded. "How about if I go on up and root around and see what I can find? I hate to try and help you up those creaky stairs. They're so steep and you'd have to hold on with both hands."

True enough. But the same could be said for him. "I don't want you up there either. Some of the flooring is a little iffy," Bailey said. She and Seth had noticed a few boards that needed replacing or nailing down while they'd been looking around.

"Is it? I wasn't aware of that. I'll need to check into it."

"We'll figure it out. It's getting a little frosty out here; I think I'm ready to go inside and sample that chili you've been telling me about all afternoon."

"I'll put the fire back on and get it warmed up for us. Joella is coming with bread and salad from work. Seth said he's got something to bring over for you, so I invited him to stay for supper."

They entered the house of her childhood and the love of the past enveloped her like a warm hug. Daddy had a Christmas tree in the corner of the family room with white lights and colorful ornaments. Bailey even recognized a few of her handcrafted ones from elementary school. There were several wrapped gifts under the tree. She hadn't taken the time to pay attention to it before when she'd been over.

Bailey could feel his excitement that she planned to stay here at the house, and that she'd be here through Christmas. There'd never been any doubt that she was his favorite person in the world, which made her feel all the more guilty that she'd deprived him of this joy so many times over the years. Yes, she'd flown him to L.A. as much as he'd agree to come visit, both on holidays and other times, but having her home for the holidays was special for him.

Bailey inhaled the aroma of homemade chili, its spices in perfect harmony, like everything Daddy cooked. Never fussy, but always delicious and perfectly seasoned. Daddy believed in leaving the cast iron pot sitting out for a couple of hours once it finished cooking with no fear of bacteria setting in. In fact, the chili was likely still very warm in that heavy pot.

The rice cooker sat on the counter with a full pot of rice

ready to go. At their house, they ate rice with their chili. And salad and bread, sometimes corn bread. Bailey's stomach rumbled. She'd eaten cereal for breakfast, but only a protein bar for lunch. Somehow between getting her things gathered and Daddy picking her up, she'd never gotten anything else.

⟫⟫⟩⟨⟪⟪

NOW, SITTING IN Daddy's kitchen, Bailey was determined to make Seth a pan of his favorite fudge with pecans. Or have Daddy help her do so.

"Looks like you're wanting to make some sweet stuff, darlin'."

"I feel like I owe Seth a pan of fudge for all he's done to help me since I've been home."

"A pan of fudge is a fine thank you, for sure," he agreed. "Since the dinner's all cooked, shall we get started on it?"

Bailey nodded, feeling her pain meds kicking in, thankfully. She reached for the bag with the chocolate.

Daddy put a hand on hers. "How about you tell me what to do and I'll be your hands?"

Bailey's inability to use both her hands proved to be far more of a hindrance than she'd predicted. And Daddy's ability to make fudge on the stovetop had proved to be far less successful than Bailey'd believed.

When Bailey had asked him where his candy thermometer was, he'd stared at her blankly. That was after he'd begun stirring the ingredients together on the burner and the mixture came to a nice rolling boil. "Okay, I guess we can try using the old water-in-the-glass method instead." Again, he'd stared at her in question. Bailey hadn't personally ever tried that method, having always had a working candy thermometer when she'd attempted such things. She'd read all about it though.

Bailey wasn't at all sure this would work with only her limited motion. But Joella, bless her, arrived just in time to save the fudge. Seth wasn't there yet, so that was a good thing, Bailey thought.

"What on earth is happening in here?" Joella asked as she looked around at the enormous mess they'd created trying to work as a team.

Bailey and Daddy both looked up at her, and Bailey imagined their expressions might have matched, perhaps slightly panicked, and relieved that Joella had arrived to save the day. Joella was nothing if not proficient in the kitchen.

"Daddy doesn't have a candy thermometer and doesn't know how to use the water-in-the-glass to test for the softball stage," Bailey explained, not admitting that maybe she didn't either.

Joella nodded. "Okay. How long has the fudge been boiling?" she asked.

"Only a few minutes," Bailey said.

"Aames, you scoot and get me a clear glass from the cabinet and fill it with cold water, would you please? Bailey, could you hand me a teaspoon from the drawer?"

Bailey did as she was bid.

Bailey and Daddy watched as Joella, with the hands of an old pro dipped the teaspoon into the hot mixture and dropped a tiny bit into the water, then she pulled the dollop back up after a second and tried it between her thumb and forefinger as if trying to roll it into a ball. "Not quite yet."

They all let out a collective sigh that the fudge hadn't overcooked.

"I've got this. Aames, you want to go ahead and put a fire under the chili and get it hot? Bailey, you can turn on the oven to four hundred for the bread. I left it on the bar in the bag along with the salad."

Joella ran a pizza joint, so she was accustomed to multitasking and delegating in the kitchen. Before they knew it, they were doing their parts to finish dinner, and Joella was spreading the newly finished fudge into a greased pan.

Seth wasn't far behind Joella. He came in after a quick knock on the door carrying her fragile Christmas tree, brought from Mrs. Wiggins's place. "Where should I set this up?" he asked.

Every time he entered a room, or approached, she caught her breath. It was like replaying a dream scenario she'd imagined in her mind for the last twelve years. She'd fantasized about it endlessly. That boy, the love of her life, who was now a man, returning to her life. A wonderful, helpful, incredibly gorgeous man. One who was still crazy about her.

"The sunroom?" Bailey suggested. Since there was already a tree in the family room, and her bedroom was upstairs, and decidedly tiny, it made sense. Plus, she liked the sunroom. It was cozy and surrounded by nature.

Seth nodded and they made eye contact. Bailey got the sensation of being in high school all over again. In a good way.

"I'll come and help."

"How about you come and tell me where to put it?" he suggested.

The two of them left their elders getting dinner on the table and went out into the sunroom, which was right off the family room and connected to the back porch. The story was that Momma had asked that they make their existing screen porch into a sunroom so she could sit out there and read and write any time of the year.

It was surrounded by windows and overlooked the back of the property, which was nothing but woods and a small pond. Bailey had had a swing set off the side of the house when she was little, but it had been fenced in so she couldn't wander off to the pond. Daddy had been so concerned about her safety that he'd made certain she could swim by age two.

Even now the room was cozy, with a braided rug, a small sofa and two chairs, coffee table, and a lamp and side table. There were magazines, so the room was used at least some of the time, it appeared. "In this corner?" Seth asked Bailey.

"Perfect." And it was. The scale of the room was smaller than the two-story family room. The tree fit nicely in the space with its lower ceiling.

"There you go." He turned after plugging it in. "I hardly remember this room."

The colored lights from the tree glowed on the walls and created a warmth that Bailey absorbed like sunshine. "Yeah. You and I didn't spend much time in here."

"I wonder why?" he mused.

She laughed softly. "Probably because there wasn't a TV in here."

"Well, that makes perfect sense. We did a *lot* of television watching back in those days."

Joella called them for dinner. "We've got a little surprise thank you waiting in the kitchen," Bailey said.

His eyes brightened a little. "For me?"

"Not a big deal, but come on, you'll see." Bailey took his big hand in her good one, noticing the callouses and how right it felt. *How long had it been since they'd held hands?* She led him toward the kitchen.

❯❯❯❯❮❮❮❮

SETH WONDERED IF he imagined it or was Bailey sending signals he'd been hoping for? She'd seemed to let down her guard since her fall. Yes, she was vulnerable right now because she'd been physically hurt, but something about her behavior toward him was new.

When she'd grabbed his hand to lead him toward the kitchen, the moment had been so natural, light and happy even. He'd not seen Bailey like that in years. And even years ago, she'd lived with such an edge to her personality, like she wasn't ever quite comfortable in her own skin. Tonight, despite her physical pain, she appeared relaxed emotionally, and without that edge she'd always carried around.

Seth couldn't allow the tiny surge of hope; there were so many barriers to both their happiness. The obvious one being the distance of a couple thousand miles. The other being the years they'd spent apart. Why was Bailey behaving like she was his girlfriend again?

"You said something about a surprise?" he teased, when they sat down at the dining room table to eat.

"Looks like you'll have to wait a little while," Bailey said, indicating the food on the table. "After dinner."

The chili Aames had simmered on the stove all afternoon diverted his attention for the next half hour from his conflicted thoughts of Bailey's strange behavior. That man could cook.

"Did you use venison for the chili, Daddy?" Bailey asked.

"Yes, I did. Had some backstrap. Gotta make room in the freezer."

"You squandered backstrap for chili?" Joella asked in a somewhat horrified tone.

"Don't you worry; there's plenty more," Daddy reassured her. Backstrap was the leanest and most tender of deer meat.

Seth had to agree with his mother; backstrap should be reserved for better use. Seth used to hunt with his daddy as a kid. Sometimes they'd be joined by Aames and Bailey. Bailey mostly sat in the stand and drew or wrote, even when they were little.

After they'd cleared the table, Bailey came out of the kitchen balancing a plate piled high with fudge with her good hand. "This was a collaborative effort, but your momma saved it from being a disaster."

"Oh my." He smiled in appreciation. "That is a nice surprise. You remembered it was my favorite."

"I hope it's still your favorite. It's a little token of my appreciation for all the times you've been there for me since I arrived in Ministry. I couldn't have pulled off getting the cast and crew settled and things ready for filming without all your help."

"Just doin' my job, ma'am." He did a fake hat tip like a cowboy might've in an old Western movie.

"I'm serious. There's no way I could've done it without you." She looked him straight in the eye then, which was something Bailey rarely did. Mostly, she'd avoided his eyes these days. Her sincere gaze affected him profoundly.

He reached for a square of the fudge, filled with pecans, his absolute favorite.

"Well, how is it?" Momma asked.

He held up a hand to silence her, then said, "I'm having a moment here," Seth said, his eyes closed in pure delight. Then he reached for a second piece. "Thanks to all of you. For not allowing this to burn or ruin, or whatever it was in danger of."

They were all now eating a square. "Yes, agreed. But next time, let's figure out a better method," Aames laughed.

"Can I help with the cleanup?" Seth asked Aames and Joella since they were the ones who normally handled it.

"No way. You can go up in the attic and get whatever it is that Bailey needs to keep herself occupied for the next couple weeks while she's sitting around here. I don't want her trying to go up there while I'm at work," Aames said with a frown. "She's forbidden me to do it because she says we've got a few weak spots in the floor up there."

Seth nodded. "Yes, sir, you do. And you shouldn't go up there alone. I'll go up and see about the floor after the holidays, but now, I'll get what Bailey needs."

He turned to Bailey. "Tell me what you're wanting from the attic."

She led him into the family room so they could talk. "I'm sorry to ask you to do one more thing for me."

Seth tried not to be offended. "Are you kidding? Of course I'm the one to go up there. And I don't mind a bit."

"Well, I guess I'll have to make more fudge, huh?" she teased.

He gently placed his hands on either side of her face, drinking in the simple joy of looking at her. Her nearness, her smell, the heat radiating from her. He wanted to kiss her so badly. But if he did, then he would need to do it again and again...

⟫⟫⟫⟨⟨⟨⟨

FINALLY. HE WAS going to kiss her. Bailey could feel his breath on her face. She wished he would wrap those big arms around her and hold her while he kissed her but she would settle for his hands on her face and his lips—oh, those finely chiseled lips.

"You need any help getting things down?" Daddy called from the other room, completely ruining the magic of their moment.

Seth closed his eyes in regret and took a step back, clearing his throat before answering, "Um, no, sir. I've got it."

Bailey grinned at him. "So, I never found my journals and all the writing I did growing up. Mostly the stuff from high school. It might be fun to see what I was thinking back then."

"You were thinking about me. Don't you remember?" Seth said smoothly.

Bailey rolled her eyes. "Well, sure, but I was writing stories. Lots of stories. And most of them didn't involve you at all."

Seth appeared slightly miffed. "Okay. Fine. Maybe not everything had to do with me back then."

She ignored that. "There were paintings and drawings too. It might be fun to see those again. And the things Momma wrote. The little books and the things I haven't had the chance to look through yet."

Seth nodded. "Okay. I'll go up and have a look."

Bailey found herself naturally migrating to the sunroom where Seth had set up the old Christmas tree. The room had such charm. There was a cane chair with a tiny matching ottoman Daddy had recently recovered with a nice light blue with white flowers that called to her. It also spoke of Joella's influence, as did many of the nice recent touches in the house.

The chair was comfy, and Bailey could tell her earlier medication was wearing off. Instead of another pain pill, she would try an anti-inflammatory this time to see if she was ready to step down every other time to a lesser painkiller, as suggested by Doctor Nick at the hospital when she was ready.

Bailey yawned. By the end of the day, she'd been getting very sleepy. Of course the very filling meal probably added to the huge yawn she was currently in the middle of when Seth reappeared, carrying a huge box marked BAILEY.

"Thoughts on where to put this?" he asked, grunting at the weight.

She pointed to a spot currently unoccupied next to a window. "I guess line them up along this wall."

A text came in from Alexis. There was a selfie of her with a cat on her lap. *No way!*

Alexis: *Miss you. Me 'n Scarlet O' Hara chillin' over here in Christmas Town. Hope you're feeling better.*

Bailey tamped down her first response to ask if Alexis was

drinking, and instead chose her emoji carefully and decided on basic heart eyes with her response.

Bailey: *Looks like a peace agreement was made between you two. Glad you've got company. Miss you both.*

After a few more minutes, Seth had brought down another two boxes and the trunk with her momma's things. "You look like you could use a glass of tea."

The sheen of sweat across his forehead was a definitive fact that he'd worked up a thirst. Bailey stood carefully. Because, pain. She tried not to grimace; she really did.

"You alright?" He was immediately at her side.

"Yep. I'm headed to the kitchen for a prescription-strength ibuprofen and a glass of water."

He held out a hand. "I'll take you up on that glass of tea."

Chapter Twenty-One

AFTER SETH AND Joella left for the evening, Daddy came and found her in the sunroom going through some old journals. They were some writings she'd done in the smelly pit of preteen existence; part daily happenings, a little poetry, and some ideas for stories she might want to write someday. Bailey winced at her twelve-year-old angst. And there *were* many mentions of Seth. He'd been right about that, as she'd known he was.

"Hi there. Find anything interesting?" he asked.

Bailey grimaced. "Depends on your definition of interesting."

"I'm glad Seth was here to help out with those boxes." He indicated them with an incline of his head.

"Yes. This should keep me entertained while I'm here."

"Well, I've got something else I want to give you. Call it an early Christmas gift if you want. It's been waiting for you for quite some time, but I decided to hold off until I felt the time presented itself. And here we are."

He handed over a large manila envelope to her usable hand.

"What is it, Daddy?"

"Oh, I forgot you can't use both hands very well." He opened it and helped spread some of the contents on the ottoman in front of the chair where she was sitting.

"Take some time and look it all over. This is yours. Your legacy. Your inheritance." He stared at her hard, unlike his usual lighthearted self, which clued Bailey in that this was a big deal.

"Inheritance?" Bailey had a moment of pure panic. "You're not—"

"No. No, I'm perfectly fine, honey." He continued, "But what good is this kind of inheritance unless you can do something with it that impacts your life while you're young? Maybe create a legacy for your children."

Bailey stared at what was in front of her, her eyes tearing up as she began to read and comprehend what this was and what it meant. "Daddy, are you sure?" Her heart sped up a little at the possibilities.

"Of course, darlin'." His own eyes filled with tears. "No need letting things go to waste when I'm hoping to be here to watch you enjoy it. It's an opportunity. It's what your momma and I planned for. I've invested wisely and this will give you some flexibility to decide your future, or at least give you some room to try on a few things."

"I had no idea, Daddy. Why now?" Bailey asked, still in shock.

"Because I sense you're at a bit of a crossroads, and I

don't want your need to earn enough to eat keep you from following your dreams."

Bailey moved forward, sitting in front of him on the ottoman. "I'm going to think hard about what to do with this." She hugged him tight with her good arm. "Thank you so much for loving me the way you do. I don't deserve it."

"Of course you do, my love. Of course you do." They pulled back. "And don't make a decision out of guilt or obligation. You are free with this. Do what you want to do with all or part of it, not what you believe anyone else wants from you."

"Thank you, Daddy."

>>><<<

BAILEY'S MIND BECAME a whirling dervish of ideas as she tore through her old journals the next day. Not that she would actually develop the stories she'd had in her teens, but it was the kick in the pants her brain needed—a reminder of the raging creativity she'd had then. The beautiful imagination Bailey had squashed since moving to L.A.

It hadn't happened overnight. Technically, her undergraduate degree was in creative writing, with a minor in film, but she had taken drawing, painting, and even graphic design courses as well. While she didn't have a master's degree, the many additional courses added up to far more than her degree called for. Bailey learned that she was a true creative, something that wasn't exactly celebrated in small-town Alabama while she'd been growing up. She'd been a weird kid to some.

But over time, as she'd grunted her way through the film business, trying to find where she best fit, her creative juices had dried up and headed for the Hollywood Hills. Bailey'd been left with a decent-paying job that took all her time and energy, but left her no real hope or desire to follow her initial dreams for pursuing this career path in the first place.

Going through the journals was like rediscovering who she was before she lost herself in adulthood. Yes, she'd been angsty and she'd wanted more. And Bailey had gotten all of it. But it had been a tradeoff. In that trade, she'd lost the most important things in her life. Love. Home. Family. Herself.

Daddy had given her something last night that might allow Bailey to regain the parts of herself and her life she believed was beyond reach. She hadn't worked it out yet, and it would be a huge change, but the very thought of pursuing something not only for herself, but for others, sparked a joy deep inside her soul.

The fall Bailey took was a strange blessing, and she planned to take advantage of it as such. But there was so much to consider, and to learn, personally still, and about how she might relate to a new environment so suddenly.

Bailey had a strong desire to discuss particulars with someone who might give her an objective opinion. She texted Alexis and asked if she could pick her up after work.

She could trust Alexis to give it to her straight.

Bailey grabbed her notepad and began making a list of the pros and cons of this idea. Why couldn't she come up with any real reason not to move forward? Besides the obvious one.

Bailey texted Seth. *I'm waiting to go on our date night. All conversations on the table. For real.*

He replied within seconds: *Tomorrow night. Wear something nice.*

A thrill worked its way through Bailey at the thought of the two of them going out alone; no Daddy and Joella to interrupt their conversation and maybe a kiss, should it come to that.

Bailey had done some hard thinking before falling asleep last night. She was ready to answer Seth's questions. She owed him that.

Last night, lying in her childhood bedroom, listening to the night sounds, Bailey had allowed herself to remember. That's something she'd not done in all her time away. Early on, she'd partitioned that pain, not letting it get through, because if she had, it would have taken her down.

Living in California as an eighteen-year-old among strangers, and away from everything and everyone familiar, Bailey had been deeply lonely for her home, her daddy, and mostly for Seth. The pain of it was physical much of the time. But she'd made the decision and she'd had to stick by it.

Bailey had been young and prideful, and determined to find her future—one that didn't involve a small town in Alabama—which meant a small-town boy in Alabama. It had never been about him though. Seth had been the most honest and true person, besides her daddy, she'd ever known. He'd loved her with his whole heart, and she'd left him for her dreams.

He'd understood because he'd loved Bailey enough to know that if she'd stayed in Ministry for him alone, she'd never have been truly happy. So, Bailey had gone away. There hadn't been a big blowup or any other reason they hadn't stayed together.

What Seth never understood was the toll leaving him had taken on Bailey. Her pride had never let her admit to anyone how much leaving him had wounded and scarred her. But then what? Go home? Not pursue the arts scholarship she'd worked so hard for her entire academic high school career? No way. That would've meant the worst kind of failure.

But she'd had to figure out how to live without Seth. So, at night, when all was finally quiet, and his beautiful face crept into her mind, to keep from dying from missing him, she'd had to learn survival techniques. Instead of alcohol and drugs, like many of her peers, she painted and listened to music. So much music on her headphones. And straight-up blocked out thinking about him.

Dating other guys didn't work. She compared them all to

Seth, so it only made her miss him more. Bailey tried to come home and avoid seeing him, but the small glimpses she'd gotten had only made it more heartbreaking, especially the time she saw him kissing Sissy.

So, she'd started asking Daddy to come see her in L.A. He seemed to enjoy it for a few days at a time, and they'd had adventures together, traveling to the Grand Canyon and other places neither had ever been.

Avoiding Seth had been essential to Bailey's ability to move forward and find her future. Over time, it had become easier to focus on school, and then on her career. It was exciting and fun to climb that ladder and realize her dreams. But this trip home—this detour from her normal life—had shaken up Bailey's belief in her goals.

The tumble on the road she'd taken had been essential for her to reimagine what her life could be. She'd lost her passion and excitement for the future, but it was now returning like fireworks exploding in the dark.

Bailey only had to figure out how to implement the steps that might get her moving in the direction of that new and improved set of goals.

SETH MADE THE reservation at *Greene's*, a new restaurant in town. It was one of only a couple fine dining establishments in or around Ministry. It served Southern food with a fancy flair, apparently. It seemed Cammie Laroux and Southern cooking maven, Jessica Greene, had patched up their differences and gone into business together.

The reservation wasn't until eight o' clock, due to the popularity of the place, and the fact that the town was bursting at the seams with Christmas visitors. Again, when Seth received the text from Bailey, he'd gotten a vibe that was different. She'd been so emotionally unavailable since arriving in Ministry that her willingness to talk now was surprising, to say the least.

But he wasn't one to miss the opportunity to spend time alone with Bailey. So far, they'd not had but snippets of time together without one or both parents around. Not that they didn't both love them, but it was hard to know when one or the other would pop into the room and totally ruin the moment.

There had been a time or two when Bailey seemed to want to open up and reveal her true thoughts and feelings. But the family interruptions had occurred at the worst possible times. And of course, there had been the almost kisses. Probably best that didn't happen in retrospect. But Seth hadn't felt that way at the time.

Bailey's and his physical attraction was on a different level now than when they were teens. Different, of course, because teen desire was intense but rasher and more oblivious, with only one goal, release.

Seth wasn't a boy any longer, and he understood his desire for Bailey now. It was that of a full-grown man. He'd dated a few women over the years and was no longer an innocent. He expected that Bailey wasn't either after twelve years. She was a full-grown woman, after all. None of that mattered to Seth. They were here and now. How she felt about him mattered. Maybe they couldn't ever be together, but it mattered.

The anticipation of tomorrow night would carry him through the next several hours of the day. The calls to the department had lately been folks asking for help finding lost pets and asking where the filming would take place next, which Seth didn't mind so much because it meant the citizens were safe. The calls he sometimes received ended in tragedy, so for now, he would be thankful for the small things.

»»»«««

ALEXIS PICKED BAILEY up around four o' clock. Bailey suggested they go to Mrs. Wiggins's place so they wouldn't be disturbed or overheard. The last thing she needed was for something to get around town and back to Seth before she was ready for it to.

"Wow, you got off early," Bailey said when Alexis arrived.

"They wrapped up early this afternoon. The Christmas pageant is tonight and they're headed over to film a short scene there later."

"Ah, the Christmas pageant. That's a big thing around

here." Bailey remembered attending to support friends.

"We didn't do that where I grew up. I mean, who ever heard of beauty pageants for little girls?" Alexis wrinkled her nose at the idea.

Bailey shrugged. "It's a Southern thing, I think. Lots of girls I knew growing up entered them. It was a big deal. There's a lot of preparation and excitement that surrounds the pageants. It's definitely something one should attend at least once before shaming the idea of it."

"I guess so. I don't have much choice, do I, since we're filming on location later this evening? I'll try to keep an open mind," she agreed. "So, what did you want to talk with me about?"

"Logistics. But you've got to keep this strictly between the two of us."

Alexis made a cross over her heart. "Got it."

Bailey began talking. They were sitting at the kitchen table in the apartment the two women had shared, so it was a comfortable setting to have this conversation.

Alexis listened, her eyes wide, clearly intrigued with Bailey's ideas.

"Wow. What would your timeline be for this?" she asked.

"I'm not sure. There are some things to work out in my personal life first. But if I can figure out a real way forward with this idea, I'm hoping that maybe by summer to at least begin. Like, in a test capacity. I would do a ton of market research of course.

"Of course. Count me in." Alexis was fairly buzzing with excitement.

"What?" Bailey couldn't have been more shocked. "You'd come and work with me?"

"It sounds like a dream, Bailey. Like something I was meant to do. If you want me, that is. I mean, we've done this Hollywood thing, right? What's the next move? This is something real and amazing."

Bailey couldn't think of anyone more suited to begin a venture like this with than Alexis. She had the analytical mind for building a business, and Bailey had the creative one. "Oh my goodness, Alexis! I can't believe I'm actually moving forward with this. But I need to talk to Seth."

Alexis took Bailey's hand. "Seth or no Seth, Bailey, I think you should go for this. We need to stop plotting our futures and our happy endings with men in mind."

Bailey nodded. Alexis had a point. A very valid and real point there. But Bailey and Seth deserved a second chance. Well, maybe he deserved one after Bailey'd left him without looking back. Bailey had taken herself from Seth when all he'd wanted was a future with her. The question was, would he give them a chance to start fresh?

If not, Bailey would attempt to make her own way. Daddy had made that possible with or without Seth.

Bailey and Alexis used many sheets of paper and made tons of notes. It did seem as if Alexis was willing to partner with her on this venture.

"I'm having dinner with Seth tomorrow night at eight, and I'm hoping we'll be able to clear some things up," Bailey told Alexis.

"So what is your history with him? I get that you two were a thing a hundred years ago, and I see the way you've been sparking off each other since you've been back here."

Bailey couldn't come up with an answer in a few words other than, "It's—complicated."

"I figured that out the first time I saw you together," Alexis said with a smile.

"We've known each other our entire lives. I've never been serious with anyone else. I mean, I've dated some over the years, but never really connected, you know?"

"Hello? Single lady here. I get what you're saying. I had a guy back home but he married someone else. At least Seth didn't do that." Alexis's expression showed her own pain at losing the one she loved most.

"I'm sorry, Alexis," Bailey said. "I honestly don't know what I would have done if Seth had married someone else."

And Bailey hadn't thought about the possibility until that moment. How much it would have hurt to miss her chance with him. Maybe she already had.

Well, tomorrow they would talk. Really talk. And she would see if her chance was still available.

Chapter Twenty-Two

B AILEY HAD BROUGHT a dress with her. It was nice. Not formal, but nice, and a deep shade of red that worked well with the Christmas theme. It fell slightly above her knees and kind of swished when she walked, making her feel feminine, despite the bandages. It was the first time since high school she'd dressed up and taken any time on her appearance with Seth in mind, besides the normal quick getting ready she did every day. He'd never seemed to need that from her.

And despite the stiffness in her shoulder, and all her still-fresh scrapes, she'd managed to put on makeup. Bailey went a little heavier on the eyeliner and mascara than a regular day. She'd paid attention to the makeup artists here and there and had learned a thing or two about a smoky eye.

Tonight was special. Bailey sought to elicit a response from him, to see his desire, and his affection. To know for certain she was still his one and only. It wasn't a tease or a test; she was serious. Bailey had to know. It was all fun and games to imagine them together as adults, but did he truly understand how that would change his life?

As she snapped the silver hoop earring in place, she winced. She'd seen Dr. Nick for a follow-up appointment today, and he was now allowing her to use a smaller, step-down sling that was less bulky. Not exactly sexy but it was meant to help her remember to not overuse her shoulder and arm.

Bailey was healing well, according to the X-ray. The shoulder tendons and ligaments were still very sore and stiff, so Dr. Nick showed her some mild movements that weren't quite stretches to help work out some of the stiffness. She could continue with the anti-inflammatory meds as needed. All in all, she was in pretty good shape.

Getting dressed was more like doing a triathlon, but Bailey preferred doing it alone. She did ask Daddy to help with the zipper in the back once she'd finished everything else.

After he'd completed the task, he stepped back to admire her. "You look gorgeous, Bailey Bean," he said, using her childhood nickname. "I'm assuming you've got a date with our county sheriff?" he beamed.

Bailey grinned, because she couldn't help it. "I do."

Groucho came bounding in, threatening to shower Bailey with affection. "No, down," Bailey commanded.

Groucho stopped in his tracks, staring adoringly at her instead. "Good boy," she said.

"That was a close one. Let's get you a treat. C'mon, boy." Daddy let him out to avoid any further mayhem.

When Daddy came back in the room, he said, "I hope

Seth takes you someplace nice, because you look like a million bucks," he said.

"We had a bet and we both won, I think. So, yes, we're going someplace nice," Bailey said.

The doorbell rang then. "I'll get it." Daddy headed toward the front door. It felt like she was back in high school.

Bailey grabbed her wool coat. Luckily, she'd thought to bring something other than her casual jacket. Living in Southern California, she had little need for jackets of any kind, but it was winter, and she'd tried to plan for weird weather here.

Seth entered, wearing a sports coat, a dress shirt, tie, and real pants. Had she ever seen him in anything besides jeans? *Wow.* He was clean shaven, and he'd clearly put product in his hair, as it had a kind of high and tight appearance. *Had he gotten a haircut too?* He had boots on, but they were what Daddy called his "church boots." Shined up without a sign of mud or muck on them.

"Hey there," he said, smiling at her. The admiration in his gaze was exactly what she'd been going for. "You look—" he took a moment to find his words while he took her in "—amazing."

"Nothing like a sling and lots of Band-Aids to finish the look." She indicated the appendage.

"I didn't notice. Believe me, it does nothing to distract from…the dress." The dress was code for her in the dress and she knew it.

Bailey rolled her eyes. She'd have punched him in the arm if she'd been less injured. "You ready?" she asked.

He held out his arm as if to escort her to the car.

Bailey took it.

"Bye, kids. Don't keep her out too late," Daddy said and winked, a twinkle in his eye.

※》》》《《《※

SETH HELPED HER into his vehicle, which had been detailed meticulously since the last time she'd ridden in it. "Your car is so clean," she said, because suddenly she didn't know what else to say.

"You haven't mentioned my hair." He ran a hand just above it like the guys did in the old movies and grinned at her.

"I like it. Very slick," she said with a little giggle at his play at coolness.

"Joe at the Beauty and Barber Barn said this is the style I should have to update my look. Said I'd let myself go for too long."

He'd been a little on the shaggy side, kind of like he'd always been, but Bailey honestly hadn't noticed. "I appreciate your effort, but I thought your hair was fine."

He frowned. "You're supposed to instantly sit up and pay attention, Joe said."

Bailey put her hand on his arm. "I'm paying attention."

"I like the sound of that. By the way, you smell nice,"

Seth said and put the car in reverse.

The short drive to the restaurant was made over small talk about how the filming was going and the bumpy dirt road. "So, it seems that Scarlett O' Hara is now a fixture on set. She's a regular at the catering truck and in the producers' trailers," Bailey said. Alexis had kept her apprised of everything happening.

Seth nodded. "Yes, I've seen her prancing around the area. They all seem to ignore her now. Except the ones who take a second to pet her. She's like a mascot or good luck charm to them."

"Movie people are very superstitious. That's probably more the case," Bailey agreed.

Greene's on the Square wasn't exactly on the square, but close enough. The Southern cooking maven, Jessica Greene, with Cammie as her silent-ish partner, had opened the restaurant last fall. Cammie was so busy with filming her show at the studio outside of town, she'd structured her part of the business as creative input instead of onsite daily operations.

The place was set off the main town square in a historic building on the strip of the downtown that used to be a department store. That allowed for parking in the back, along with a rear entrance, Bailey noticed. Downtown strip parking was a rare find, especially this time of year.

Greene's was decorated for Christmas with all clear lights and garland. The walls were white-painted brick and the lighting was somewhat dim and romantic. They checked in at the hostess stand and were greeted by a well-dressed young woman in a Santa hat. "Right this way, Sheriff McKay."

Their table was tucked away in the corner, which suited Bailey fine. They looked at the menu and ordered a bottle of wine and tap water. "This is very nice. Ministry's come a long way," Bailey said, and meant it.

"Yes, it has. Tourist traffic is a mixed bag though. The economy here has improved, which helps employment, but it has an effect on our overall small-town culture."

"In what way?" Bailey asked, truly interested in what was bothering him.

"Big corporations are starting to take notice of the uptick in our tourism. They are nosing in on our small businesses. Trying to buy up blocks of our historic homes for development."

A lead weight dropped in her gut. "Oh, no. That's horrible."

"So far, we've been able to block the tearing down of the protected historic homes through the historic home registry. Those can't be touched. But nothing prevents them from buying real estate that's not protected and building big box stores and condominiums."

Bailey frowned as she pictured Ministry becoming exactly like everywhere else. "I can't bear the thought of it."

"I know," Seth said. "I guess that's what we get for our progress." He indicated the restaurant by gesturing with his hand. "But Ben and I have been working on some legislation and hope to at least slow the big stores from coming too close to the city limits."

"Keep them a little farther out and less convenient to customers? That way, the mom and pops still have a chance," Bailey said. "Great idea."

The waiter brought their wine and they tasted it before she poured. It was a very good Pinot Noir.

The menu was somewhat simple but it was hard to choose, being that everything looked delicious. "I'm interested in the jalapeno pimiento fritters as an appetizer. Have you had them?" Bailey asked. Yes, it was fried cheese, and yes, it was a Southern thing.

"Sounds good, and no, I haven't. But I have had the rosemary roasted chicken, and it's fantastic."

"Ooh, look at the creamed corn and fried okra. I definitely want those for sides."

"Sounds like you're hungry."

"Starving. And don't think you're getting off easy. Appetizer, dinner, and dessert. Oh, and this lovely wine too," she teased, but then said quickly, "unless you want me to pay half, because I am happy to." It had just occurred to her that she had no idea how he was set financially. She'd simply assumed he was okay.

He grabbed her hand and stopped her rambling. "Bailey, I'll be paying for our dinner, even if you order everything on the menu. Got it?"

She nodded, breathing a sigh of relief at his reassuring tone and manner. "We've never discussed your finances is all. But I mean, why would we, right?" she said, a bit awkwardly.

"Let's order, why don't we?" he suggested.

They both went back to their menus. "So, what do you think about this shrimp n grits? Or maybe the meat loaf and mashed potatoes?"

"I think we're going to end up with a lot of to-go bags if you don't narrow it down," he said. "I think I'll try the fried catfish strips with horseradish remoulade and hush puppies."

"Ooh, that sounds heavenly. I'll get that with a side of creamed corn."

They ordered as soon as the waiter came by and sipped wine a bit awkwardly. "Why are you now worried about my finances?" Seth asked.

"I'm not, really. I mean, I expected you to pay for my dinner without making sure you were up for it, I guess," Bailey said.

"How about you not worry about that. I'm fine. There's a loft above the sheriff's office downtown that's very spacious where I now reside. Before that, I lived in Momma's house. She's alone, so it's worked out. But I've always made money and saved. I own land, I've got a degree, and I'll always have a job here."

"I didn't mean to imply otherwise, Seth, really," she said softly. "How much money you have means nothing to me."

He frowned at her.

"I said that wrong, didn't I?" Bailey groaned. "Seth, I wanted our evening to be special." She took his hand in hers. It was warm, and weathered from working outside. "I want to come home, Seth, to live here again."

He pulled back as if she'd shocked him with a cattle prod.

"You what?"

Bailey would have sworn he was angry.

"I-I have an opportunity to start a venture—a business at Grandview."

"So, you're coming back home for Grandview?"

She teared up; she couldn't help it. "I was hoping you might give me another chance."

"You and me? Like, date each other?" His voice quavered, as if he were on the verge of tears as well. "Are you serious?"

A tear fell from her left eye and rolled down her cheek. "Seth, I haven't been able to move on without you. I tried. I went to college; I worked hard and told myself I was chasing my dreams, but I lost sight of what I truly needed. Love. You."

"Why? Why now? After twelve long years? Lost years?" he demanded, agony in every word.

She grabbed his hand in hers on top of the table. His precious hand. "I nearly died from hurting when I left you after high school. I was so lonely, but stubborn and determined to find a new life; one without the stigma of a motherless girl in a small town with no future. One where people understood me. But it didn't work. It wasn't better out there. I've grieved you the entire time I've been away. Since I've been back here, every single day has been a gift of healing and love for me."

His face crumpled. "Bailey, all I've ever truly wanted was you. I love you."

Tears were unashamedly streaming down her cheeks now. "Can you give me a chance?"

"I've spent every day that you've been back here doing whatever I could to prove to you how much I cared. My heart is yours. Please don't break it again."

"I love you, Seth McKay." They both leaned in and finally indulged in the kiss they'd been waiting for.

Their food arrived at that very special moment, and somehow they ate every last bite.

Chapter Twenty-Three

THE COOKIE AND candy swap took place as it always had in downtown Ministry, Alabama. Alexis and Bailey (as much as she could) helped Mrs. Wiggins bring down her many tins and plates piled high with shortbread. It appeared that every person, both men and women, came with offerings to share. It was a gathering of friends and neighbors. And this year, it was being filmed.

"Cut. And that's a wrap," the director yelled. There was applause and hugs between all the cast and crew, and pretty much everyone nearby. Bailey avoided the hugs as much as possible due to her still-sore shoulder, but she was included in their celebration, as were the townspeople swapping cookies and candy. It was a festive night in the town square, with the massive and colorful tree standing sentinel, while all around them was the beauty of the town and its lights.

Seth found her among the revelry and handed her a hot chocolate. Bailey took it from him and grinned. "Thanks." The moment reminded her of the tree lighting right after she'd arrived in town. But this time he put an arm around her and they walked together, an obvious couple.

This was her home, and Seth was her guy, just as he'd been for so many years before. It had taken so long for Bailey to find her way back to him. He was happy, and it thrilled her to watch his transformation. He laughed easily and seemed so relaxed around her now, whereas before, he'd been a little tense.

And tomorrow night, they would gather around the Christmas tree at Daddy's house and open presents together, a family. And next year, they would do all this again, minus filming a movie. And again, the year after.

Epilogue

D ADDY, ALEXIS, SETH, and Bailey stood outside the cabins at Grandview. Hollywood had wrapped up filming last week. They'd paid for cleaning, so that had been done the day they'd cleared out. This Christmas had been the best of Bailey's life.

Now, it was time to figure out how to accomplish this new venture. Bailey planned to breathe new life into Grandview. It would be a children's camp for the arts: music, writing, visual arts (drawing, painting, and other mediums). Daddy had handed over the keys and the ownership of the property. She could make of it what she chose.

Bailey immediately foresaw what she'd missed in her own childhood: a safe space where kids could let their creativity flow. She'd had to stifle it in Ministry because it wasn't the norm. Bailey had felt like a "weirdo" running around with her notebook, writing stories. Only the kids who'd excelled in sports and beauty pageants were celebrated for their talents and beauty, or so it had seemed.

This town had come a long way since then, but this plan of hers, a program for kids like Bailey had been, might help normalize their gifts and allow for more young local artists to thrive here instead of running off to find their dreams like Bailey had done.

Epic Studios had given her a substantial grant for scholarships to disperse to underprivileged deserving students. They'd done so when Bailey had resigned her position with them. It was a thanks to her for saving the movie filmed here in Ministry.

Apparently, things had gone incredibly well, and they'd finished early and under budget. The studio executives had traced that to Bailey Boone's quick thinking and organizing the move for filming in Ministry. When they found out about her plans for the arts camp at Grandview, they put their money where their mouth was and made the donation.

"There are already accommodations for wheelchairs. I made certain of that when we built the place," Daddy said. "But the codes and standards now might be somewhat different than they were thirty years ago."

"Got it." Alexis added it to her list of items. Alexis would be the details' person, while Bailey would be the creative director, determining the kind of curriculum and who the staff would be. Those hires would be vital.

"You know that there's a huge liability insurance policy to run a business beside a body of water," Daddy said. "I've paid an umbrella note over the years, but less since the kids don't come anymore. You'll have to shop around for that."

"Got it," Alexis said.

Bailey's excitement was boundless for this new project. It would have most of the elements for summer camp, too, because, who didn't love summer camp? And kids, in her opinion, didn't get enough of that experience these days. Plus, it would be an art immersion, which meant no devices during the day and during certain times in the evening, like during meals and guitar playing beside the campfires and s'mores time. Kind of old school.

Summer camps were still popular in lots of places, but this would be different. Hopefully, she could sell it. Alexis would be awesome at promotion, along with whomever she hired to do an amazing website. Daddy had given her the money and the Grandview property as her legacy. And she planned to make it a roaring success.

And well, there was Seth, who'd decided they were going to be a roaring success as well. Bailey had never, and would never, meet a man who was a better match for her. He loved her in a way that nobody else ever would, and she could appreciate her love for him after their years apart. So deep and so true, Bailey now understood her momma and daddy's love for one another.

The End

Want more? Check out Cammie and Grey's story in Again, Alabama!

Join Tule Publishing's newsletter for more great reads and weekly deals!

If you enjoyed *Noel, Alabama,*
you'll love the other books in the....

Alabama series

Book 1: *Again, Alabama*

Book 2: *Love, Alabama*

Book 3: *Forever, Alabama*

Book 4: *Christmas, Alabama*

Book 5: *Noel, Alabama*

Available now at your favorite online retailer!

About the Author

Susan Sands grew up in a real life Southern Footloose town, complete with her senior class hosting the first ever prom in the history of their tiny public school. Is it any wonder she writes Southern small town stories full of porch swings, fun and romance?

Susan lives in suburban Atlanta surrounded by her husband, three young adult kiddos and lots of material for her next book.

Thank you for reading

Noel, Alabama

If you enjoyed this book, you can find more from all our great authors at TulePublishing.com, or from your favorite online retailer.

TULE
PUBLISHING

CPSIA information can be obtained
at www.ICGtesting.com
Printed in the USA
LVHW091330230921
698567LV00016B/234